ALSO BY THE SAM

The Villagers

DI Claire Falle series

Lonely Hearts

Home Help

Death Bond

Dr Harrison Lane series

Preacher Boy

The Horsemen

Dark Order

Holy Man

Writing as Gwyn Garfield-Bennett

Islands

404

PLEASE NOTE: SPELLINGS USED IN THIS BOOK ARE BRITISH ENGLISH.

Published in 2021 by Chalky Dog Publishing

THE HORSEMEN

GWYN GB

CHALKY DOG
PUBLISHING

1

He wasn't sure which emotion was in control of his body. Nerves or excitement. He suspected they both had their part to play in his slightly wobbly legs and the betraying squeaks coming from his stomach. He was standing in the graveyard, next to the headstone marked Robert Henry Lester, just as he'd been told to do.

It was dark. Apart from the fact it had just gone midnight, the moon was only a thin strip of white struggling for attention behind black clouds, which seemed to have gathered above him in readiness for something. His eyes had started to adjust to the lack of light, but that had in some ways made it worse. All around him shadowy gravestones rose from the ground, while the whispers of the breeze came at him from all directions, carrying rustling and scratching sounds which hinted at the fact he wasn't alone.

He felt them, but only a split second before they were upon him. The distinctive dusty smell of hessian covered his head and hands grabbed both his arms. He gasped for air as his heart beat wildly and he stifled the urge to shout and run.

'We are The Horsemen,' said a voice. 'Do you wish to become one of us?'

'Yes,' he croaked out, throat tight, mouth dry, but mind made up.

Two men guided him, one on either side, gripping his arms and leading him back through the churchyard.

Gravel on the path under his feet.

The squeak of the wooden gate as they exited.

Then through the weave of the hessian bag over his head, he saw some light, and he was half pushed, half guided into what he guessed was a car seat.

All this time, the men around him were just footsteps and breathing. They didn't say another word until they'd reached their destination. The inner sanctum. Then the chanting began.

Now there were more of them. Voices all around him as they led him into whatever place they had arrived at. Flickering lights. Candles maybe?

The constant, steady beat of the chant.

A loud knocking as something was banged on the ground in front of him. It made him jump and silenced the room.

They pulled the hood from his head.

In front of him was what appeared to be an altar, candles on either end, but it was the man who drew his eye. Wearing a black hooded cloak and with a white wooden mask of a horse's skull on his face and head. In his hand, he clasped a large wooden staff with horns on the top and a hoof on the bottom.

'Are you here to swear allegiance and brotherhood to The Horsemen?' the figure asked him.

'I am,' he replied. The hairs were raised on the back of his neck and his palms felt sweaty, although he wasn't hot. He dared not take his eyes away from the figure, but in his peripheral vision he could see others sitting around him, their faces also hidden behind the white masks of wooden horse skulls.

'Is it of your own free will?'

'It is''

'And who vouches for this man? Who will swear he is worthy and well qualified?'

A figure stepped forward from his right side.

'I will.'

'Then the candidate must kneel and the initiation ceremony commence.'

2

The fact it was a Saturday was both good and bad news, depending on whose viewpoint you considered. For Detective Sergeant Mark James, it was good because it meant Dr Harrison Lane had a couple of days off and might just agree to help him. For Harrison, if he agreed, then his plan to get out of London and head to the New Forest for a spot of walking and getting back in touch with nature, would go out the window. The only positive was that DS James was from Cambridgeshire police, and while it meant pointing his Harley in the opposite direction, he was at least going to escape the city.

'It's just bizarre,' the DS was explaining. 'The way we found his body, and the horses… If it leaks to the press, we'll be swamped, and the nature reserve will be flooded with nutters wanting to see if they can find some kind of spiritual connection. I need answers now so I can work out what we're dealing with.'

Harrison listened to the DS's voice grow slightly more breathy as his anxiety levels ramped up. He stared out of the enormous windows in his Docklands apartment. Outside, the Thames flowed brown, and the sky showed the promise of rain. It wouldn't be a great weekend for walking and enjoying the views, anyway. There'd probably be mist or fog by the time he got to the New Forest.

'Is the body still in situ?' he asked. He liked to review the scene as untouched as possible.

'Yes,' Mark replied eagerly. 'Forensics are still working. It's going to be at least another two or three hours before we can move him.'

'OK. I'll be there.'

DS James ended the call with a sigh of relief. He wasn't sure if the lack of conversation reflected Dr Lane's mood at being called on a Saturday, or his reputation for going about things in a somewhat maverick manner. Either way, he was glad that in a couple of hours the head of the Met's Ritualistic Behavioural Crime Unit would be standing by his side. Harrison's reputation for helping solve bizarre cases was something he could be sure of.

It was the deep guttural sound of the Harley Davidson that first alerted Mark James to Harrison's arrival. He was stood on Burwell Fen, part of the Wicken Fen Nature Reserve. They were at least a good forty minutes walk from the visitor centre and so Mark had given Harrison directions to meet them at the intersection of Priory Drove and the aptly named Harrison's Drove which sat on the other side of the National Trust land. Although Harrison had to park up a good five minutes walk from him, the engine noise carried. There was nothing to soak up the sounds. In front of him was the flat landscape of the Cambridgeshire Fens. The only structures breaking the neat line of endless sky were the electricity and telephone pylons along the edges of the Fen, and the occasional cluster of trees.

He was on the outskirts of an area once marshland, where peat and reeds had been harvested for centuries, battles fought and lost. Kings and monks hid from advancing armies, and the final battle between locals and noblemen took place as the Duke of Bedford, aided by a Dutch engineer, started to drain the Fens in the 1600s with a series of ditches and dykes. A couple of centuries later, in 1899, Wicken Fen became the very first National Nature Reserve in England. It was still beautiful, but today an icy shiver had settled in DS Mark James's spine. His mood reflected the slate grey heavens above, but it had been brought on by the sight that had greeted him when he arrived. A small herd of the wild Konik ponies that grazed the Fen, seemed to be standing vigil over the body. They'd been forced to move away now with all the activity, but not so far that he couldn't still see them staring. It felt like the ponies were watching their every move.

Mark had brought his children here countless times, to ride their bikes, run around looking for butterflies, and to wear them out in the fresh air. He was glad they weren't here today. Fortunately, it had been an adult who'd come across the remains of the man. It had been obvious the death wasn't natural.

Dr Harrison Lane strode towards him. Even from a distance he looked imposing. Wide, angular shoulders in a black leather jacket. A few centuries ago, he'd have been the kind of man that you'd be hiding in the reeds from if you didn't know him. Mark walked forward slowly to greet him. The police incident line was behind him, a large area cordoned off and guarded by officers waiting for forensics to give the all-clear before a fingertip search could be undertaken. He wasn't too optimistic. It had rained heavily in the night, evidence would have been washed away or deteriorated, and the herd of wild ponies had already trampled the ground.

'Dr Lane?' He reached his hand out in greeting. The man in front of him was muscular and tall. If he'd an image in his head of what a doctor of psychology and ritualistic crime might look like, he was definitely not it. Short black hair and a thick neck led down to a body which wouldn't look out of place on a cage fighter. The small brown eagle tattoo on his neck added to the overall effect. Still, he came well recommended.

'DS James.' He nodded back.

'Thanks for coming, I really do appreciate it. He was discovered this morning by one of the reserve staff. We don't think that—'

'If you don't mind I'd rather you let me look at the scene before you tell me what you think. It prevents any confirmation bias.'

DS James found himself with his mouth half open. He closed it. He didn't know what to say next.

'Could I be allowed to view the scene alone?' Harrison asked. 'It helps me focus on the facts and evidence.'

They'd come to stand at the edge of what was clearly the controlled zone. A box of forensic over shoes and suits was on the floor next to a uniformed officer with a clipboard. Behind him they had erected a tent over the site of the body. The threat of further rain and a brisk breeze necessitated the protection of any remaining evidence. It also prevented the countless rubberneckers, attracted by the police activity, from seeing the victim. DS James had seen several pulling out their phones and taking photographs, no doubt for a social media update which would inevitably bring the local media here before too long.

'Er, yes, let me speak with the crime scene manager,' DS James replied and putting on a fresh pair of over-shoe covers, headed off towards the tent. If he was honest, he felt relieved to step away from Harrison Lane. Although he was the Senior Investigating Officer and in charge here, the man made him feel like a rookie. There was a commanding presence about him which, despite the open landscape, seemed to fill the air. It was both unsettling and reassuring at the same time.

3

Harrison Lane stood just inside the designated police cordon, forensic overshoes and suit on. Almost all the investigating team were behind him, but the crime scene manager had insisted on staying close to the body to ensure there was no contamination. He'd never heard of Dr Harrison Lane, and he was damned if he was going to let some stranger compromise his crime scene.

Harrison walked forward a few paces and stopped. He needed to clear his mind, channel his focus after the ride up. Cars and motorway miles still flashed through his head. The beat of heavy rock guitars reverberating between his ears. He closed his eyes and breathed in deeply, feeling his muscular chest fill with fresh air and his shoulders relax. Harrison caught the scent of peaty earth, the faint odour of still water, and a hint of horse dung. He stood rooted to the ground and tipped his head slightly for the wind to blow directly into his ear, rather than allow the cascading cacophony to rush over its surface. Now he could pick out individual sounds. There were birds not too far away. Their calls similar to those you'd find on the seashore in winter. The breeze rattled tree branches to his right, the rustle of dry leaves and creak of wood. Tall dry grasses bent in the wind. Underneath all this was the sound of the ground itself. The porous soft peat had a life of its own. You could almost hear the water soaking into it, the occasional pop as a bubble of air or gas escaped. Harrison felt the steady beat of his heart, the rhythmic in and out of the air in his lungs. He tasted the fresh air, flavoured with thousands of years of organic matter, compressed into an earthy sponge. He tried not to think of the generations who had stood here before him, their history all around, but instead rooted himself firmly in the here and now. Only once the Fens had filled him, from head to toe, did he open his eyes again, ready to see.

Harrison didn't look at the scenery, or the threatening skies, he dropped his eyes to the ground. There was a clear path marked for personnel to travel to and from the body, and another area that was out of bounds. Harrison stopped and looked at the track of footprints which were marked and protected on one side. They were dug into the soft soil and pointed towards the body. Some were obliterated by a thick tyre mark which ran through their middle. He knelt and looked more closely at the tracks, comparing depth of footprint to his own. His eyes focused along the trail to the forensics tent, and he stood back up, but didn't follow their lead. He'd been given permission to walk where he needed and instead, he began a large clockwise journey around the area, not once taking his eyes from the ground.

A clump of small trees held his attention for a while and here he picked up more of the footprints which led to and from the site of the body. This time without their tyre mark companion. The closer he got, the more horse's hoof marks there were. Finally, he came alongside the edge of shallow water. There were tall grasses along its shore and occasionally he stopped and looked where these had been bent and broken.

Into the forensic tent and in front of him lay what looked like the body of a boy in his late teens, spread-eagled, face down. His skinny torso wore a Berghaus waterproof jacket, and water covered his lower legs, which were clad in jeans. The body had been roughly strewn with branches, as though somebody had attempted to hide it. Underneath the platform that forensics had placed around the body, Harrison could see a second set of footmarks. Almost certainly those that belonged to the ranger who'd discovered the corpse. The clear indicator, apart from the branches, that this had been a deliberate act, was the large iron horseshoes, one of which pinned the dead man's left wrist to the ground. They'd been used like staples, only it was highly unlikely that the victim would have been able to attempt an escape. These weren't meant for that purpose in life. One of them lay to the right side where somebody had attempted to roll him over, presumably to check for signs of life.

Cause of death was almost certainly related to the ligature marks around the man's neck. From the angle of them and the burns, it looked like a hanging. Harrison took one last look and then stepped back outside. A thin mist of rain had started and was patterning the surface of the water, creating a whisper of a dance. In the far distance he could see a row of trees large enough for the man to have been hung, but nothing close. His weight would have snapped the thin branches of those he'd looked at earlier, before death had its chance to claim him. From the evidence he'd seen so far, this didn't surprise him.

Harrison's brown eyes narrowed. He needed to see more, but for that the body would have to be turned over so he could examine it.

DS James waited expectantly at the edge of his crime scene, watching Dr Harrison Lane pace, head bent, around it. The pathologist had just arrived, and he too was pacing impatiently in front of him, waiting to go in, muttering about being busy and having someplace else to be. As soon as Harrison looked to have finished, Mark gave Dr Andrew Marshall the all clear to head to the body. He needed an approximate time of death asap, as well as confirmation of ID and mode of death. The rest he needed Harrison Lane to work out.

Inside the small forensics tent, Dr Andrew Marshall crouched beside the victim, watched by two forensics officers, DS James, and Harrison.

'Rigor mortis present in the entire body. Cooling will have been impacted by his light build and having been left outside overnight, but I'd say you're looking at some time around midnight. Ready to turn him over?' Dr Marshall asked his audience.

Carefully, they flipped the body on to a plastic sheet that had been placed alongside, on top of a board that would be used to carry him to the white morgue transport van. Once there, he'd be reacquainted with Dr Marshall. The sheet would be used to protect the body and ensure any evidence which came with it was retained and not lost to the surrounding mud.

The ground was so wet that although there was a layer of mud on the victim's face; it was thin and watery enough for Harrison to see that he was a man and not the teenager his body had first indicated. His face wasn't the purple he'd have expected from the blood settling after lying face down post-death. It was wax like. He looked almost inhuman, a plastic mannequin discarded. It was obvious to all those present why his pallor was so pale and transparent. There was a deep hole where the man's heart should have been. Someone had ripped his top open so that it looked like he was only wearing the black waterproof jacket, making the contrast of his skin even more pronounced.

There were two other things which drew Harrison's eye. The first was the rope burn around his neck, and the crucial clue was the small V-shaped bone hung around his throat on a leather string. It started to make some sense.

'My God!' exclaimed DS James. 'They've cut his heart out. It's Paul Lester, the jockey.'

Another clue for Harrison, but he needed to check one more thing.

'Could you look in his pockets for some kind of small bottle that's perhaps been smashed or broken somehow?'

The forensics officers looked at him nonplussed, and then at DS James. He nodded at them to do as Harrison had asked.

'Look for some ID, would you, and his phone too?' Mark added.

Carefully, they felt inside the man's jacket. There was nothing in the front pockets, but as they opened up his jacket to look inside, Harrison smelt it. The others did too, although they didn't know what it was.

'Careful,' Harrison said.

'Are you expecting a dangerous substance in the bottle?' DS James asked.

'No, the contents are safe. I'm just concerned it might be glass.'

The female forensics officer slowly put her gloved hand inside the first inner pocket. It was empty apart from a tissue which she placed in an evidence bag. Then she checked the final pocket, but withdrew her hand quickly as though she'd been burnt.

'There's broken glass in there,' she said and looked to Harrison for instruction and with a little admiration for the fact he'd known it was there.

'Thanks, that's all I needed to know.'

Those around him exchanged further glances and the odd eyebrow raise, before continuing with carefully bagging the victim's hands to protect any evidence under his fingernails and getting the body ready to move.

Harrison stepped outside the tent. A few moments later, DS James joined him.

'You're onto something?' he asked. 'How did you know there'd be a broken bottle?'

Harrison was staring off towards where they'd parked, deep in thought. He ignored the DS's question.

'He wasn't killed here,' he said, turning to look at the detective beside him. DS James looked like he hadn't slept much last night. No time to shave this morning, and his shirt underneath his suit wasn't ironed. He'd obviously been pulled out of bed early to come to the crime scene.

'The marks on his neck. Could be strangulation, but could be hanging. I've got officers checking the area,' he said.

'I'm pretty sure you'll find he was hanged, but not here. At least, not anywhere close. He was brought here. There are footprints which lead from the lane. He was carried in some kind of wheelbarrow. You can see the tyre print.'

'I know where he lives. We'd better get round there next, see if that's our murder scene. What's with the horseshoes and the cutting out of his heart?'

'He's a Toadman,' Harrison replied.

'Toadman?'

Harrison suspected more, but at this stage wasn't 100 percent sure, and so he chose not to share anything more with DS James. They needed to focus on what was fact.

'Toadmen are part of the folklore around here.'

'Folklore! What's that to do with a modern race horse jockey?'

'It's not unheard of that some people revive the tradition,' Harrison replied.

None of this was making sense to DS James. 'Are you saying it's some kind of cult killing?'

'I think someone who believed he possessed magical powers killed him and brought here him. Someone who believes in witchcraft and the so-called pact with the devil that Toadmen are sometimes assumed to have.'

'OK, you know what, I've no idea what you're saying here. We need to get to Paul's address. He lives alone. After that, we need to head back to the incident room and brief the team. Could you come with me and give us a briefing? We all need to understand what this is about.'

Harrison nodded. He could tell DS James was highly sceptical. The detective started walking, then stopped and turned to him.

'You're sure of this stuff, right? It's going to sound like a load of hocus pocus nonsense to my team.'

Harrison smiled.

'It is, unless you happen to believe in it and then it's very real.'

'OK.' DS James nodded, but Harrison waited. There was something else on the police officer's mind. It showed in the furrows of his forehead and the set of his lips, and it was the reason he'd called him here, despite his sceptical views.

'The ponies.' The detective nodded towards the group of horses which they could still see, silhouetted against the grey light of the sky. 'It's weird. They were here when he was found and haven't left. It's almost like they're standing guard over the body—' His voice trailed off. He wouldn't have said that in front of his team, but it was the same words the ranger and first police officer on the scene, had used. It had given him the creeps, especially now he knew the victim was a jockey. Harrison smiled.

'And that, DS James, is exactly the kind of hocus pocus trickery that makes people believe they're seeing something they're not. I'll follow your car on my bike.'

Mark James found himself left with his mouth half open for the second time since meeting Harrison Lane. He was teasing him. He knew it. He silently cursed the man, but quickly followed his fast receding back.

He couldn't see the curve of a smile that had appeared on Harrison's lips. He'd put the DS out of his misery at the briefing.

4

Harrison followed Mark James's unmarked car through the lanes that surrounded the Fen and closer to Newmarket. They drove through the village of Wicken, which began with an uninspiring collection of modern bungalows and old style cottages and houses. The Methodist chapel stood at the roadside, neat and simple in its faith. Further on and a quaint village green and pub appeared on the left-hand side and, as they exited the other end of the village, the houses became more affluent and established. The stone Church of England building rose up on the right of the road, that was flanked by graveyards. They were neat, tidy places of burial, understated and open to the skies, not like the overgrown Victorian grandiosity of Nunhead Cemetery that haunted

Harrison's mind. He pushed those thoughts away. He needed to stay focused on this case.

Then mile on mile of flat farmland, brown and green patchwork, edged with sage coloured woollen clumps of trees. Through this landscape, the A1123 was carved. Into Soham, a town forever darkened by the murders of two young girls in 2002. They travelled on into a light industrial area with warehousing, before once again trees lined the road. DS James's car turned off and took smaller roads and cut-throughs. It was clear he knew this area well, weaving through the countryside without hesitation. Before long, large properties with immaculately fenced paddocks started to appear on the outskirts of Newmarket, and the telltale white rails of gallops showed through hedging.

Mark James indicated, and they pulled in through large gates, carrying a stylish black and white sign that declared they were entering Three Oaks Stables. Paddocks ran either side of the entrance drive. To his right, Harrison saw mares with gangly legged foals. The youngsters' ears pricked and rotated to the sound of his bike engine. Then they bucked and gambled around their mothers, who had stopped their grazing to watch the strange beast throttle into their domain. A few scenarios flashed through

Harrison's mind. A horse bucking off its rider, another panicking and escaping onto the road. He reduced the bike engine to its minimum and looked for the first place he could pull over and park up.

DS James disappeared between two large barn ends, which Harrison guessed would be full of horse boxes. He pulled the Harley over and took off his helmet, before walking the rest of the way into the yard. A dozen horse heads on either side turned in his direction, their breeding and pedigree evident in the line of their noses and sheen of their coats. He was obviously of no threat or interest because they soon tossed their heads and looked away, or disappeared inside their dark boxes. He spotted Mark at the other end of the yard, just getting out of his car.

Harrison had barely walked halfway through the yard towards him when a man in a Three Oaks Stables jacket and baseball cap appeared from the end of the block.

'Can I help you?' he asked. 'Do you have an appointment?' He addressed Harrison only and didn't even glance Mark's way.

Harrison presumed the man knew well enough he didn't have an appointment. The question wasn't said rudely, but it was loaded in readiness for whatever came next; and the look on his face said he didn't think Harrison could possibly have any business being in his yard.

He looked at the man. Around the height of an average jockey but with more weight on him, still a whisp of a man compared to his own solid, muscular frame. He was spotless, not a scrap of hay dust or horse hair on him, and he was clearly used to being in control. Harrison weighed him up. He didn't have the confidence and authority of an owner, but was obviously a manager of some form. The man was about to say something else when Mark walked up to them.

'Scott.' He reached out a hand to Harrison's inquisitor.

'Mark, good to see you. You, after Richard?'

Harrison noted the red tinged fingertips of a nail biter. It was immediately obvious the men knew each other well.

'I am. Is he at the house?'

'No, the pool barn.'

'Thanks, and this is Dr Harrison Lane. He's with me. Harrison, Scott Smith, is Head Lad here, I won't keep him long, Scott.' DS James moved off round the end of the left barn and Harrison followed.

Scott barely acknowledged him, but took Mark's word and seemed placated by what he'd said. If he'd been a Jack Russell terrier, Harrison would see the fur on the back of his neck starting to flatten, and the growling cease. Before he disappeared round the end of the barn in Mark's wake, Harrison watched as Scott walked over to one of the boxes and flicked the bolt head down flat. He wondered if that was a reflection on the horse or the man.

'Scott runs the place like clockwork,' qualified Mark, as he pushed open the door to a large modern barn. What greeted Harrison was not what he'd been expecting. A huge oval pool filled the barn, and two horses were swimming along on opposite sides, both in head collars and leads, a groom walking along with them outside of the pool. In the middle of the pool was a man in green corduroys, a jumper and flat cap, standing on a raised platform above the water. All three wore Three Oaks Stables branded jackets. The man in the centre of the pool turned to see who had entered.

'Mark!' He raised a hand in greeting. 'To what do we owe this pleasure?'

'Richard, I need a quick chat. Here in my professional capacity I'm afraid.'

Richard's face changed and Harrison could see his eyes scanning Mark's and checking his own for some signs of what they might be there for. He gave some instructions to the two grooms and then placed a drawbridge over the pool to step across and down onto the barn floor so he could walk towards them.

'What's this about, then?' he said as he drew up to them. He was a man who clearly led an active outdoor life. Healthy skin over a body that didn't appear to carry any excess weight, but he enjoyed his life. The laughter lines around his mouth and eyes were evidence of that.

'This is Richard Carter, successful racehorse trainer, owner of this stable, and my cousin,' Mark said, turning to Harrison. The unspoken meaning of the latter statement, in terms of the investigation, was clear on Mark's face. This was his first SIO role, and now looked like it might be his shortest. If their murder victim was in any way connected to his cousin, then he wouldn't be able to continue with the case for conflict of interest reasons. It was also obvious that Mark wasn't going to let go of the reins just yet. He'd have to be absolutely sure there was a conflict first.

'Richard, this is my colleague, Dr Harrison Lane, from the Met police. Let's go somewhere more private,' Mark said, leading his cousin with a hand on his back, out of the pool barn.

'We have reason to be concerned for the welfare of Paul Lester,' he started.

Harrison knew he was treading carefully. Next

of kin hadn't yet been informed and ID positively confirmed. Mark was absolutely certain it was Paul, but they didn't want this leaking out yet.

'Paul?' Richard spun round in surprise. 'Saw him yesterday. He was on good form. Took one of the horses out on exercise in the morning. Haven't seen him today.' He looked at his cousin. The men clearly knew each other very well because it didn't take him long to realise that Mark had to stay tight-lipped. He didn't push the point.

'We need to take a look in his cottage, if that's OK?' Mark said gently.

'Sure. I'll get the spare key, give me a minute.' Richard walked off towards the large brick-built house which ran along the northern border.

Harrison waited with Mark in the yard. The DS was on his phone and checking in with the team for updates, while Harrison looked around him. There were security cameras in several places. He calculated they were situated to cover every inch of the place. Racehorses were expensive beasts and nobody wanted another Shergar.

As he stood there, the two horses which had been in the pool were led past him, clip clopping on the tiled yard floor. Water still dripped from their bellies, veins bulked across the surface and down their legs. Muscular thighs rippled in wet skin. They were beautiful animals. In top condition, athletes of the equine world. The grooms individually led the pair into two stables with large lights in the ceiling.

Richard came back to see Harrison staring at the last horse's rump disappearing into its box.

'Solarium. It warms and dries them after the swim,' he said to him. 'Here we go.' He turned to Mark, holding out the keys.

Harrison carried on taking in this strange new world around him, one where horses went for an afternoon swim and chilled out in solariums. He wondered if the stables offered them massages and manicures, too.

'The CCTV cameras, do you keep recordings?' Harrison asked.

'Yes of course. We've got ten of them covering every inch of the yard.'

'So they'd have captured Paul coming and going?'

'No, unfortunately. There's another lane the cottage uses for access. We don't want unnecessary traffic through the yard.'

Harrison nodded.

'The cottage is this way.'

They walked behind one of the barns, past a smaller building which said 'Tack Room' and round the back where there was an old hay barn tucked away that had been converted into staff accommodation. The conversion was an old one, and the building looked tired. Harrison thought back to the horses in their state-of-the-art boxes, while their grooms had to make do.

'We've just started some renovation work on the staff accommodation,' Richard said to the men, as if he'd heard Harrison's thoughts. As they rounded the corner, a pile of builders' materials was in front of them.

'I'm impressed by the high standards of accommodation your horses have,' Harrison said.

'I'm a little OCD when it comes to the horses.' Richard smiled. 'But you have to be. They're put in my care and some of them are worth hundreds of thousands of pounds. We have to be on top of everything.'

They walked round the back of the hay barn, to where there was an area of paddocks. Across these, Harrison saw a small cottage, sat on its own. This was their destination.

'Where does Paul keep his car?' Mark asked his cousin as they walked.

'Out front. It's always here when he's at home.'

Mark and Harrison both knew Paul wasn't at home. Question was, where had he parked his car because it wasn't outside the cottage.

'Thanks, Richard, we'll take it from here.' Mark smiled reassuringly at his cousin and put his hand out for the key. 'And please, not a word to anyone. Not until we've confirmed a few things and spoken to Paul's family.'

'I don't understand it,' Richard started, obviously upset. 'He has everything to live for, he's doing really well. I mean, I've seen the pressure get to some of the lads, you know the need to keep their weight down and keep on winning. But Paul, he's talented. A rising star.'

'I can't say anything, Rich,' Mark said quietly.

'Of course, of course, but if we can do anything, you know if you need a search party or something, I can raise a lot of people.'

'Thanks, we'll be back in touch. Someone will be along to interview you.'

Richard nodded and turned to leave. 'I'll be at the house.'

They waited for him to head back, and then Mark and Harrison walked the last fifty yards alone.

'He's a good bloke, you know,' Mark said. 'Built this place up into one of the top yards in the country out of almost nothing.'

Harrison knew why he was saying it, and it was why he also knew Mark wouldn't be running the case for much longer. He changed the subject to save him any further awkwardness.

'Does he own the tracks over there too?' Harrison nodded across the far paddock to where a long straight grass track could be seen stretching into the distance. A small group of horses were just visible, bunched like ants following a trail back to their nest.

'No, that's the Jockey Club Estate's training gallops. All the trainers use them, they've got two and a half thousand acres of grounds around Newmarket. The town revolves around racing, there's something like eighty trainers based here. You can't move without seeing a horse.'

The conversation broke the awkwardness, and it wasn't long before they'd arrived at the cottage and walked behind the hedge which separated it from the narrow lane. There, the DS handed Harrison a forensic over suit, boots and gloves.

'I don't have my body cam because I came straight from home, so I'm going to use my mobile phone camera. I'm glad you're here. You're an independent witness in case some smart-arse lawyer tries to rule out any evidence we might find in there inadmissible because of my relationship with Richard.'

Harrison nodded. Mark was right. He needed to cover all eventualities.

Once they were both suited and booted, Mark switched on his mobile phone video and started recording.

'The time is 3.51 p.m. on Saturday 2nd October. Myself, Detective Sergeant Mark James of the Major Crimes Unit, based out of Huntingdon, and Dr Harrison Lane, from the Met's Ritualistic Behavioural Crime Unit, are about to enter the property of Paul Lester, who we have reason to believe has been murdered.' Mark scanned his phone camera across to Harrison, and then back to the front door of the cottage. As he stepped forward with the key to open it, both of their hearts were pounding, ready to face the bloody evidence of Paul's demise.

5

Pools of sticky dark red blood coloured both men's minds as they pushed open the front door with gloved hands and carefully entered. They were met by the sight of a hallway bordered by a row of riding boots in various degrees of cleanliness and age. Riding crops and whips poked out from their tops, and here and there were other detritus of horses and riding, including a pile of saddles. The hallway carpet wasn't exactly hoovered and spotless, but it showed no signs of a bloody exit, just mud and the odd fleck that looked suspiciously like it could be horse manure. Photographs and paintings of horses, some antique, covered the walls.

Harrison let DS James lead the way. He would

have liked to hold back and walk around alone, to focus, but he knew Mark was relying on him to witness the fact he hadn't tampered with anything in the house. He couldn't let him out of his sight.

In front of him, the DS was giving a running commentary to his mobile phone video recording. They stepped carefully around, touching as little as possible. By the front door, Harrison noticed a dish with loose change and supermarket receipts in it. He suspected it was probably where Paul would also toss his car keys when he walked through the front door. There was no post stacked up, and it didn't look like the local free papers or junk mail made it to this out-of-the-way cottage.

In through a door on their left. The sitting-room. A rectangular shaped area that would look just like anybody else's lounge areas if it wasn't for the huge bookcase at the far end that was weighed down with horse racing cups, trophies, and ribbons. On the wall in this room was also a large framed photograph of Paul atop a winning horse as he'd just crossed the finish line, arms raised in triumph, his steed's nostrils flared, muscles pumped.

Mark was videoing some plates and glasses on the coffee table in front of a large wide-screen TV. Paul had been entertaining. Harrison's eye was caught by something on the sideboard. A leather-bound book. He crossed the room to take a closer look. It was yet more proof of what he already knew. There were only about ten other books in the room, 'Seabiscuit: An American Legend', by Laura Hillenbrand and A.P. McCoy's 'Winner. My Racing Life', plus a selection of books on horse care and management.

Using a pen from his pocket, he poked at some paperwork nearby in the vain hope it might contain some further evidence of what he also suspected. It was just various correspondence from the Jockey Club and courses around the country. A bronze sculpture of a prancing horse served as a paperweight to more paperwork. He didn't want to touch it before forensics had been in, and anyway, they looked like more of the same.

The size of the TV, a discarded PS3 box, and latest iPhone box on the floor all gave Harrison the impression that this was a man who had started to come into some money. It fitted with what Richard said, that he was a rising star. That would raise suspicions of a jealousy motive, but Harrison knew otherwise. The person who had cut Paul Lester's heart out hadn't done it because he was jealous.

The room was moderately untidy, a classic

bachelor pad that hadn't seen the swipe of a duster or been visited by a vacuum cleaner in some time. That meant no attempt at a cleanup. The murder scene hadn't been in this room.

They moved back into the hallway and to the end of the corridor, which led into the kitchen. The moderate mess theme continued. Paul obviously hadn't been a regular one for washing up, and there was nothing to suggest a struggle or any other criminal activity. Four dirty mugs were on the side, all with various horse related cartoons and photographs on them. When Mark looked in the kitchen cupboards, there was only one clean mug and a few wine glasses left.

The kitchen was small, with basic facilities, and the fridge contained only a few things. A calorie-controlled fish pie, a bag of carrots, and a couple of apples, with almond milk, and a clutch of eggs in the door. On the table were several copies of the *Racing Post* and a skull cap without a silk cover. A washing machine sat flashing at them, a batch of clean clothes finished and ready to be emptied. In front, another pile of dirty jodhpurs and jeans were waiting for their turn. There was no doubting a jockey inhabited the cottage. Wherever you looked, there was horse paraphernalia. To Harrison this wasn't a man who just loved his job and saw the animals only as beasts to ride, he seemed to have a great deal of respect for them. He also had obviously not intended to be away for any length of time.

They started up the narrow staircase, the wooden steps creaking with their weight. At the top, they were faced with just three doors. Mark went to the left, which turned out to be the main bedroom. A double bed with its blue tartan duvet thrown back dominated the room. Clothes were across the back of a chair and in piles on the floor, while a wooden wardrobe held what looked to be the smarter clothes a rising star jockey might need, including a black dinner suit and bow tie. Harrison crossed to the window and looked out. The view was across the paddocks and to the staff accommodation block. The top windows were clearly visible. From here, he could also see where the renovation works were taking place to the roof. He made a mental note to get Mark's team to find out if any of the staff had seen anything unusual going on at Paul's cottage yesterday.

Harrison carried on scanning the room while Mark took the video and looked for any signs that could indicate a murderer had been there. Nothing stood out. Everything looked as you might expect it to.

Then Harrison saw it. The proof that he'd

been after. On Paul's bed was an envelope with nothing written on it except 15:00. It looked empty, but when he got closer, he saw a long thick black hair poking out. Paul had clearly thrown it onto the bed before he'd left and after getting up yesterday. Next to it was a pair of riding jodhpurs. He'd got changed before going out. That fitted with what Richard had said about Paul riding out with them in the morning.

'Mark,' Harrison said, interrupting his commentary. 'We need to bag that envelope and hair, it might be key.'

Mark followed Harrison's line of gaze and swung his phone camera around to look too. He turned back, frowning.

'An empty envelope?'

'It's not empty. It's a message, an invitation. There's a horse tail hair inside. We need it secured.'

'OK,' Mark replied, although his voice didn't sound convinced. 'Hold this, would you and film.' Mark handed Harrison his phone, and he watched through the small screen as Mark took out an evidence bag and tweezers and carefully put the envelope and hair inside.

The second door turned out to be a small box room. The spare bed was unmade and in here were more trophies—presumably the lesser important ones that didn't merit public display downstairs. Mixed in with them were Pony Club photographs of a beaming little boy holding red rosettes. Paul had obviously started young. The last door led to a small bathroom and toilet. It was a good option for someone who wanted to commit a bloody murder, but it was in the same state as the rest of the house, moderately clean. It was obvious that nobody had committed, or tried to hide, a murder in here. There wasn't a speck of blood or bleach.

'OK, so I think we can safely assume he wasn't murdered here,' said Mark, as they pulled the front door closed behind them.

'It will be somewhere like a barn, which is away from other buildings,' Harrison said. 'An old traditional barn rather than a modern structure.'

Mark stopped and looked at him.

'How could you know that?' he asked incredulously. 'There's no way you could work that out. He could have been killed anywhere.'

'He was summonsed. That envelope you have was the invite. He got changed before he left. He would have gone to a barn, and that's probably where he met his killer.'

Mark still didn't look at all convinced, but there was no time for him to argue.

'Let's get back to the incident room and brief

the team.' He looked at Harrison through narrowed eyes. 'Are you ready?'

'Absolutely,' Harrison replied and headed back to his Harley. It was always the same when he worked with someone for the first time. Mark would learn.

6

'I'd like to introduce Dr Harrison Lane, head of the Met's Ritualistic Behavioural Crime Unit. He's kindly agreed to give up his Saturday to review our victim and circumstances and has some—' Here DS James paused momentarily in front of the dozen-or-so expectant police officers and support staff. It wasn't such a long pause as to alert the room, and most importantly his boss, DCI Robert Whittaker, that he had started to have serious doubts about how he and the rest of the team were going to receive the next ten minutes.

Harrison saw it.

'Some interesting insight into how and why Paul Lester was killed.' Mark nodded to Harrison for his cue and gave him a look which almost pleaded with him to be kind. Not to mention too much about toads and witches. For his first SIO case, why couldn't he have had a simple drug gang hit, or domestic, why did he have to be given a well-known body on the Fens with a herd of horses standing vigil over it, and a connection to his cousin? He thought he'd at least pulled a trump card by getting such a well-respected expert involved, but now his face told a different story.

Harrison didn't share the DS's nerves. Most people would experience some kind of activity in their stomach right now at the prospect of standing up and talking to a bunch of strangers—and potentially strangers who were indifferent, if not downright belligerent, towards what he was about to say. The anxiety and expectation in the speaker's brain would travel down the superhighway of the vagus nerve to their gut. Dr Harrison Lane was well used to sceptics and smart-arses. He knew that his nickname back at the Met was the 'Witch Doctor'. He also knew he was dealing with the human mind and scientific facts. Both of which he was comfortable with.

It wasn't arrogance that kept his stomach still or helped him stand up and start talking with a steady voice. It was confidence. He knew what he saw, and he understood the motivations behind it. He had, of course, studied Freud and Piaget, Carl Jung's model of the psyche, and in particular the shadow and its relation to evil. Damasio's emotional decision making and Wason's confirmation bias. He'd considered the placebo effect, cognitive therapy, psychosis and evolutionary, and behavioural psychology, cognition and gender identity. He'd also studied societal beliefs and rituals, religions and cults, from the early days of man to modern times. The fears, the devotions, and the blind beliefs that shape human behaviour. The biggest fear of all was the unknown, whether that be what happened after death, or the fact Cambridgeshire police were dealing with a secret society of Horsemen who, probably for traditional reasons, and a sprinkling of hope, believed in the magical power of toads and lore passed down the generations. Harrison got on with it.

'The victim, Paul Lester, is a horse racing jockey. He's fairly early in his career but has had two good years which means he's now in demand. I've already read several interviews online where not just his expertise with horses, but the bond he seems to have with them, has been mentioned and that's an important fact to bear in mind.'

So far, so good. The men and women in the room were all still watching and listening. Now to get onto the interesting stuff.

'He was killed by somebody who believes he

used magical powers to control horses.' There was a gentle ripple around the room at the mention of magic. 'The first clue to this is the bone around his neck.' Harrison looked behind him to a photograph on the board of the small bone attached to the leather cord.

'What? A wishbone?' one of the female detectives said and then looked as though she hadn't meant to say it out loud and pulled her lips together in an attempt to reel it back in.

'It's not a chicken wishbone,' Harrison said to her reassuringly. 'It is, in fact, the ilium, or pelvic bone of a toad.'

The officer raised her eyebrows but listened intently.

'Folklore said that if you took the body of a toad and put it into an anthill until the flesh was eaten away, then threw its skeleton into a stream or river, the bone which floated up would give you power over animals and even people. The details of the practice were highly secretive, passed down only by word of mouth. Very little is written about it but some believed those who carried out this ceremony also made a pact with the devil to get those powers.'

Harrison had emphasised the word *believed* and looked to DS James. He could see this was completely out of his comfort zone, but he pressed on.

'It's superstition of course,' he confirmed, and saw the detective's face relax a little. 'Horses were incredibly important in the times they believed this. The lands around here relied on them for ploughing and there were the Ploughmen or Horsemen societies which sprung up among those who cared for them. The Horsemen often used toad bones to control their horses and it was a secret society. You had to undergo an initiation by invitation only. Those in this inner circle were a bit like what we'd consider horse whisperers nowadays. In reality, it's thought these societies had the best interests of the horses in mind, they probably shared information on best practice as well as protecting their own incomes. But they were also revered by ordinary people for their so-called powers.'

'Great history lesson, but how does all this relate to our victim?' An older detective spoke up now. He was in his early fifties, a smoker, or ex smoker, and a heavy drinker. Harrison could see the telltale results of both habits on his skin, the smoker's wrinkles around his mouth and the inflamed skin of too much acetaldehyde, the byproduct his body produced from alcohol. He suspected the latter issue was why he was still a DS and working under Mark at this stage of his career.

'These Horsemen societies are revived now and then, and it's been known for young apprentice jockeys, desperate to further their careers and immersed in the horse world, to also revive the Toadman ritual. Paul Lester was doing well. He not only had the bone around his neck, but in his cottage, I saw a copy of the book, *The Toadman* by Nigel Pennick. That's a limited edition, toad skin bound book which describes the practice of toadmanery and costs around a thousand pounds. He took it seriously. Then there's the scented oils. He carried a small bottle of a mixture which I suspect was irresistible to horses.'

DS James looked shocked at this.

'It's been thought for a long time that one secret of the Horsemen related to using scent to control. Horses have excellent senses of smell, not as good as dogs, but far better than ours. There are certain scents which are attractive and certain ones which repulse them. When Paul was found, there was a herd of wild ponies around him. They appeared to be standing vigil over his body. I smelt something unusual and a broken bottle confirmed my theory. They'd been drawn there by a scent. To anyone who didn't know about this trick, it could seem magical. It certainly would have spooked the killer. They probably started gathering shortly after he'd arrived on the Fen, perhaps interrupting his disposal plan. To him, it was evidence Paul was controlling them from the grave.'

Harrison turned round to the images of the Fen behind him.

'Paul was summonsed to where the Horsemen hold their rituals and meetings. It's likely to be a barn, away from other buildings, and traditional in style. He was hanged and his heart was cut out. When you find the killer, you will find the heart. It's been taken as a form of protection against what the murderer thinks is Paul's magic powers.'

There was a murmur around the room now.

'The body would have bled out and was then transported to the Fen by the killer to dispose of it away from consecrated ground. He wasn't a particularly strong man. He took the body from his car via a wheelbarrow. The iron horseshoes placed over Paul's wrists were there to prevent him from rising and going after the killer. Iron was thought to be a metal that stopped bad spirits, as too are the branches of birch which were gathered and placed over the body. They weren't to hide it, they were to protect the man who had brought him there. He was spooked when he saw the horses come to stand around the body. You can see that in the pattern of his footprints. He ran from that scene.'

'So, we're looking for a madman who believes in magic?' One of the officers spoke up. 'Surely he should be easy to spot.'

'Whoever killed Paul believes in the powers of the toad bone and the Horsemen rituals, and I think they're still very scared. It will be fed by superstition and fear, but there might be your standard human motivations for crime behind it too. It's almost certainly someone in the horse racing world, perhaps a rival. The shoe size is quite small, it fits with somebody who is shorter than average and not a heavy build. I'll write up a profile for you, but for now I'd concentrate on the places Paul works. The usual tensions you would investigate. He will be an obsessive, compulsive personality, quite possibly openly superstitious, and display ritualistic behaviour. There are others who might know or have suspicions, such as the members of the secret society of The Horsemen. Find them and they could lead you to your killer.'

'You think one of these Horsemen could be the murderer?' the female detective asked him.

'It's more likely to be someone outside of their circle. They're all privy to the same secrets, and in theory the same powers. This is somebody who sees Paul's success and puts it down to the magical secrets he has. Somebody who's frightened by those powers, or perhaps wants them for himself. But I have concerns. We need to wait for the post-mortem, but how did the murderer manage to hang Paul? He's light, no more than about 115 to 120 lbs, but so too is the person who brought his body to the Fen. A little heavier, probably at around 140 lbs, certainly smaller than an average male. How did he overpower him and then lift him enough to hang him? There is something, or perhaps somebody, missing which we can't yet see. It could be simple, like he was drugged, but I'm not so sure.'

'How can you be so sure about the size of the person who took his body there? It could be more than one person. Or it could be a woman.'

'There's only one set of footprints, they're small and the depth of the imprints in the peat show they're not heavily built. The only other footprints belong to the ranger who found the body and the first responders. Despite the churned ground around where Paul was found, because of the horses, you can see that in the approach to it.'

'Dr Lane has tracking expertise,' DS James jumped in. He could see the suspicion on the faces of his team and he'd done his homework on

Harrison. He knew all about how he'd been brought up by a Shadow Wolf, one of the elite Native American trackers who patrol the borders of the USA and Mexico for drug runners. It was often one of the most helpful factors on a case because he could immediately see signs that it would sometimes take the forensics teams days to confirm.

'As for being female?' Harrison continued, 'I'd say highly unlikely but in theory, not impossible.'

'Why hanging?' another detective asked. 'Is that significant?'

'It was a common mode of killing witches, along with burning at the stake and sometimes drowning, although the latter was usually as a result of an attempt to see if they were indeed witches. Hanging and burning were post-sentencing. It's also said there's a fake hanging as part of the Horsemen's initiation ceremony. It could be related to that.'

'Nice…' the detective replied. 'And you really think that in our modern society there's someone who believes all that stuff?'

'Oh yes. Trust me, I come across them every day.' Harrison smiled. 'Many are mentally ill, or under the influence of drugs, but some are what we might think of as being completely sane.

Power, faith, and money are tremendous motivators.'

'OK, thank you, Dr Lane,' DS James jumped in. He needed his detectives out there and on the phone, not discussing the methods of killing witches or practicing folklore. 'As I mentioned, we've been to Paul's cottage and there are no signs of suspicious activity, although he had been entertaining and Dr Lane asked me to bag something he felt was significant. We've got forensics over there now. Any signs of his car?'

'Not yet, sir,' a young constable spoke up. 'But there was no mobile phone on the body and we've just received the tracking data for it. It's still switched on. They've sent me over the triangulation coordinates.'

'Let's get them up on the screen then,' DS James said eagerly.

The young officer walked up to the laptop and typed in some information, and a map appeared on the TV screen in front of them.

'It's between these three mobile masts,' the young officer said.

'That's Fordham Woods in the centre,' one of the team spoke up.

'It's going to take us a while to search and it's getting dark.' DS James's face had dropped.

'Sir, I walk my dog in those woods,' the

detective constable at the back of the room said. 'There's an old barn on the outskirts, on the Newmarket side. Dr Lane said the murder site could be an old traditional barn away from other properties. I'd say that one fits the bill exactly.'

DS James threw a glance at Harrison. 'OK, take a colleague and get over there pronto. I'll get a search team up and running in the meantime, but if you strike lucky, let me know.'

Mark James wrapped up his briefing and waited for his boss, DCI Whittaker, to walk towards him. This next bit was going to be the painful part.

'Interesting briefing, Dr Lane. Thank you for assisting us with this,' DCI Whittaker said to Harrison, extending his hand.

'Sir, could I have a word,' DS James said, ignoring whatever the DCI meant behind his choice of the word, *'interesting'*. 'I have something I need to talk to you about.'

Harrison felt for Mark. His shoulders already showed the disappointment that was about to be landed on them. He sat at the desk he'd been shown to earlier, and got on with writing his report on who he believed the team should be looking for, and the reasoning behind it. He knew that after DS James's chat with his boss, the case was likely to take a new turn. In the meantime, he'd do what he'd come there to do.

Fifteen minutes later, DCI Whittaker came back out of his office and walked over to the detective in his early fifties, the one who'd spoken up earlier in the briefing. Harrison sighed. Maybe his time here had been wasted after all. If he was Mark's replacement, he couldn't see him taking his advice seriously. The pair walked out of the incident room together, deep in conversation.

Moments later, the call came in that the murder scene had been found. The barn on the edge of Fordham Woods had a large pool of dried blood on its floor, and a hangman's noose lying close by. At the news, it was like someone had stirred up a bees' nest. All around him, the room began to buzz and swarm. Progress. Perhaps now they'd find their killer.

Harrison knew he'd done all he could for the day. Forensics would need to get into the barn and seal it off, which would preclude him from taking a look just yet. With the rain hammering against the window like it had for the last hour, there was no way he was going to try to get back home tonight. He had a hotel room booked anyway, and tomorrow he'd see if his services were still required.

7

Harrison checked into the Premier Inn and went straight to his room for a shower. The room looked clean enough. Every establishment had upped its game since the Covid pandemic swept the world. Amazing how even an innocuous television remote control was now seen in a different light. How many hands had touched it, and had they been washed? Many people, certainly those over a certain age, viewed the world through Covid tinted glasses now, seeing potential hazards where before they wouldn't have thought twice. The remote wasn't an issue for Harrison. He rarely turned the TV on. He also didn't need luxury, but he wasn't keen on some modern budget hotels because invariably the windows were small and wouldn't open at all or would only open a fraction for safety reasons. Consequently, the first thing he did was turn off the heating. The room felt dry and overly warm. If he wanted to sleep tonight, he needed cool air.

This was the first time today that he'd been able to stop and let his mind rest. Viewing a crime scene was exhausting, a bit like doing a giant dot-to-dot puzzle when you didn't know which of the dots in front of you should be included. He was presented with a myriad of clues and useless pieces of information, and he had to work out which were the critical gems, and then connect them together. It involved all he had learnt about psychology and criminal profiling, tracking and the vast bank of ritualistic and religious behaviours that humans had practiced over the generations. He had to ask, what had taken place to cause the person's death? Who was involved, and what motivation or belief had led to the consequences he was now investigating?

He got undressed and went into the bathroom, wrapping a towel around his waist. For a moment he lent on the sink, staring at the man in front of him. His eyes looked bloodshot, tired from the ride up and the detailed examination of the crime scene. Harrison rubbed his face, feeling the hard bones of his jaw underneath a fresh scattering of stubble. His neck sloped into smooth broad shoulders, with his clavicle bone a curved ridge topping the bulk of his pectoral muscles. There wasn't an ounce of fat on him, but although he had barely eaten today, he didn't feel hungry. Focusing on work often had an appetite killing effect, possibly helped by the usual hazard of having to look at the remains of people who'd met their ends in often quite unpalatable ways.

Harrison pushed himself upright off the sink and saw his triceps flex and ripple. It reminded him of the horses today at the stables and he felt the urge to exercise and test his body; to feel the energy coursing through his system. If he'd been at home, he could have gone on his treadmill, or run along the bank of the River Thames, pushing himself until every muscle screamed and his lungs hurt with each breath. He'd come away without anything suitable to wear for a run, but he could at least do some endurance floor exercises: abdominal crunches, push-ups, and planks.

For an hour, he squeezed and flexed his muscles, controlling his breathing, focusing on overcoming the pain threshold. As the air in the room grew cooler, his body got hotter, building up the sheen of a sweat, until the veins rose on the surface of his glistening skin, just like the racehorses he'd seen earlier. Finally, he'd had enough. He knew a hunger would soon arrive in his stomach, and sleep would come easier this evening. Harrison had his shower, enjoying the hot water on his body and the endorphins settling into his brain from the exercise as they relaxed him and brought a sense of peace. Nature's feel-good drug.

He wasn't oblivious to what he was doing, and the reasons why. Harrison was able to analyse the behaviour of murder suspects and decipher their motivations. He was just as capable of analysing himself. The need to keep pushing himself to his limits, exercising to exhaustion, and the absolute fear of being distracted. He was terrified of failing. Terrified of losing control. A natural loner, but he did get lonely. He craved love, but he rejected it. He believed that if he allowed himself to fall for someone, then it would cloud his mind, alter his instincts, and prevent him from tracking down his mother's killer. Nothing could interfere with that. It was his entire reason d'être for everything he'd done with his life. He wouldn't let her, or any other victim down again.

Harrison contemplated room service, but the thought of having to eat in the small room, cramped on the tiny table and then the lingering smell of stale dinner, drove him to head down to the hotel restaurant. He left his aubergine furnished room with its plain purple carpets for the patterned wood flooring of the downstairs communal areas and breathing space. At the entrance to the restaurant, a young woman, probably about thirty, greeted him. She appraised the handsome man in front of her within seconds and decided that the evening had just got a lot more interesting.

'Table for one?' she asked with the tilt of one eyebrow, as Harrison took a pump of the hand gel.

'Yes, please,' he replied, and hoped that she wouldn't keep trying to hold a conversation with him. He'd brought an academic paper to read. It was interesting new research into the evolution of African witchcraft and how it had morphed into focusing on targeting children. The woman didn't look like it was a subject she'd be interested in. She had no wedding ring on and her make-up and hair had been carefully prepared. Harrison felt like a deer under the gaze of a leopard. He didn't want attention, he wanted to meld into the background and not be seen. Perhaps he should have ordered room service.

The young woman showed him to his table. She chatted away pleasantly about her day and asked him if he was something to do with horse racing or here as a tourist. He answered as economically as possible without being rude, and asked to be seated as far away from other diners as possible. He didn't want their conversations interrupting his thoughts, but he didn't tell her that. Today's case was attempting to dominate his mind again. There was something he couldn't quite see which niggled him. A missing piece to his solution. A dot that eluded him and left a line dangling. He hoped that the murder scene might throw some light on the answer and that he could get access to it tomorrow.

There was something about these hotel restaurants, the ones only frequented by travellers and never locals on a night out. It was the anonymity of the atmosphere, like a masquerade ball where you could be anyone you wanted to be. You could present yourself as your alter ego and nobody would know any different. It was a liberating feeling, a disconnect between the here and the realities of responsibility which awaited you at home. Harrison recognised that feeling and knew it to be a compulsive one. It didn't last long.

He'd just sat down when his mobile phone buzzed to tell him a text message had been received. Harrison was expecting it to be Mark James, but instead Dr Tanya Jones's name flashed up. *Hi, are you around this evening?*

Harrison's heart and stomach gave a little jump in unison. Tanya was a woman who threatened his resolve. One of the lead forensic officers back in London, they'd worked together on a big case recently, and he'd been impressed with her on more than a few levels. He knew Tanya was worried about a potential stalker, and he'd made a promise to be there for her if she needed him. His personal interest was stifled by concern for her welfare.

Out of town in Newmarket. Is everything OK?

He was waiting for her response, for the status bar to tell him she was typing, when the waitress came over to ask him if he was ready to order a drink.

'Sparkling water, please,' he'd said.

'You don't want a beer or a glass of wine?' She encouraged.

'No. Thank you,' he replied firmly, keeping his eyes on his phone screen in the hope she'd get the message.

Tanya was typing. The waitress left. Harrison wondered if he should offer to ride back to town.

I'm fine. No worries. Let me know when you're back. I'd appreciate your opinion on something.

Harrison breathed in relief. It was probably something to do with work.

Back tomorrow afternoon. Give me a call.

Will do. Enjoy your weekend.

As he put his phone down, the waitress

returned with a small bottle of fizzy water and a glass. 'Are you ready to order your food?' she asked, smiling into his eyes. The message hadn't got through.

'Sorry, I was just texting my girlfriend,' Harrison replied. He didn't want to be cruel, but he was relieved when he saw the slight downtick of disappointment on her face. He skimmed the menu. 'The sirloin, please, medium rare with salad.'

'Any sauces with that?'

'No, thank you.' Harrison picked up the academic paper from the table and turned the page. He looked at it, but he didn't see it. He had allowed himself to fantasise. His mind had an alternative scene in play, one where he was sitting at this table with Tanya opposite him, chatting. Her blue eyes would be looking into his from under their curtain of thick, long lashes; and her full lips, which often wore a hint of pink lipstick, would be smiling. Tanya's porcelain skin would be framed by her long brunette hair and the light would be just catching some of the golden highlights, making individual strands shimmer as she moved. He could almost smell her perfume. In his mind's eye, they would enjoy their meal before returning to his room together. He had to get a grip. Harrison forced his eyes to focus on the paper in his hand, almost testing himself about what he'd just read to ensure his brain was processing it. He needed to keep his knowledge up to date. He had a job to do and there was nobody else in the country who could do it like him. He had to keep focused.

8

In London, Dr Tanya Jones stood in her kitchen, still holding her mobile phone after sending the text to Harrison. It had taken her a minute to press the send button on a message that was the exact opposite of what she actually wanted to say. She stared at the card in the plastic evidence bag in front of her. To most people, it was an innocuous thing, a pink card with hearts that read: *To my wonderful wife on our 1st anniversary. Our love story will never end.* It would be a nice card to get if you were happily married, but Tanya wasn't. She wasn't even in a relationship. She knew the card was from him—her stalker—but she had absolutely no idea who 'him' was. Needless to say, it hadn't been signed.

The second she'd opened it and realised what

it was, she'd bagged it for evidence; but if she was right about this man, he knew exactly what she did for a living and so the chances of finding any identifying forensic evidence on the card or envelope were going to be slim. She suspected the only DNA she'd find was from the postman who'd delivered it.

Right now, she'd dearly love to know that Harrison was on his Harley heading her way, but there was no way she was going to drag him back to London just because she'd received a card. She wasn't that pathetic.

Tanya had told him about the stalker when they'd worked on their last case together. In her head she'd rationalised telling him because he's a psychologist. At first, she'd thought the stalker had all been in her own mind. In her heart she also knew she'd told Harrison because she'd like nothing more than having him around looking out for her. He was a good-looking man with a fit body, what wasn't to like? But Tanya wasn't some air head who just went for handsome, it was inside the head that counted. Harrison intrigued her. He was intelligent, confident, independent, and scientific in his approach to life. A sure-fire magic potion for her to fall in love with. Problem was, he didn't seem to feel the same way. Occasionally there was a connection that she thought was stronger than just colleagues. She'd glimpsed a bubbling, overwhelming passion in his eyes that she knew could consume her whole; and which she'd gladly give herself up to; but then it would disappear and an invisible barrier would return.

She'd tried to make discreet enquiries. Was he gay? Had he been married before? Had he experienced some kind of awful trauma in a relationship? The answers were all negative and Tanya discovered that Harrison Lane was a hot topic of coffee machine whispers among the single women at work. Many had tried before her and failed. Right now, she would make do with having his attention in a professional capacity. She needed him to get inside the head of whoever was stalking her and help work out who they are and why they won't leave her alone.

Tanya had been out with friends for lunch, a fun catch-up at a new noodle bar just down the road. Four of them had gone, all friends from Strathclyde University where Tanya had studied forensic science. The choice of Strathclyde had been a decision driven partly by the strength of the course, and partly by the desire to put a few hundred miles between Tanya and her mother. Her parents lived in Gloucestershire and to be fair, they were great parents, it's just her mother was a little smothering. She was an only child and suspected her birth had been hard won. They'd doted on her but at eighteen, Tanya wanted to fly the nest and establish her own life and when she realised her mother was trying to persuade her to apply for universities that were close to home, she suspected an ulterior motive and rebelled. She hadn't regretted it, and now their relationship was great, her mother had discovered painting, and when her father retired early, he'd become the focus of her mother's need to look after someone. He hadn't complained.

Lunch with her friends had rolled into afternoon drinks and by the time four-thirty rolled around, they were all somewhat tipsy. Tanya wasn't good at afternoon drinking, when they'd left the restaurant, and the cab had dropped her off at home, she had a vision of crashing out on the sofa for a couple of hours, watching some crap Saturday early evening TV and then shoving a ready-made meal into the microwave.

As soon as she stepped out the cab, she felt him. It was so hard to explain. Perhaps it was expectation. She was convinced he watched her home, but in reality, she'd never seen him or had any idea from where he could be watching. For a long time, she'd told herself that she was just imagining it. Perhaps something in her day job had spooked her and filtered through her brain's defence mechanism into her own life. Then the flowers had started arriving. She hadn't told Harrison that part yet. It was usually a single rose posted through her letterbox. That meant he'd been there. He knew where she lived, and he knew when she was out. Tanya had doubled the locks on her doors and bought herself a panic button, CCTV, and rape alarm. She started feeling like she was under siege.

The worst part was not knowing who he was. Did she just walk past him down the street? Her usually bright and friendly nature had started to change, and she was avoiding men's eyes. The crazy thing was she worked for the police, but that also afforded her the knowledge of how difficult charging people for this kind of thing was. Now, he'd escalated. He'd shown her that he felt she was his by calling her his wife. She was scared.

When the doorbell's shrill ring burst into the silence of her flat, she jumped, her heart banging in her chest. As the heavy fist banged on her front door, just feet from where she was standing, she dropped her mobile phone on the floor.

9

They were sweating, and it wasn't even 8am. Four of them had been trying to load the horses onto the truck ready to take up to Doncaster, and the last one wouldn't budge. They'd tried every trick in the book, including bribery, trickery and shoving. They'd stopped for a few minutes because the animal was getting stressed and when you were dealing with valuable highly-strung horses, that was not what you wanted.

'He's always been a right bugger to load,' one lad said, folding his arms and looking at the horse with disdain.

They'd lent against the wall, thinking what to do next when Sam walked round the side of the truck.

'Having a problem?' he said as he handed the paperwork over. Sam was a large muscular guy, originally from Ghana, where he'd worked with polo ponies. Sam was not welcome here. It had nothing to do with his ancestry and race, and everything to do with the small bone hung around his neck.

Sam nodded to the horse, which stood, eyes warily watching every move they made. Hooves firmly planted on terra firma.

'Want me to try?' Sam asked.

'You're OK, we'll figure it out'.

'If you've got any suggestions we need all the help we can get,' one of the lads interrupted, overhearing the conversation.

Sam threw a glance.

'That horse is getting stressed. I don't want him hurting himself on my truck,' Sam said. He wasn't going to take no for an answer.

Jaw clenched to prevent anything they wanted to say from coming out, they watched as the big man walked over to the horse, approaching him slowly. The animal flared its nostrils and looked straight at Sam. They willed it to rear up and strike the man dead, but knew that wouldn't happen. There was a greater force protecting him.

Sam held out his hands for the horse to sniff, and then gently moved in and allowed it to nuzzle him, as he stroked it and talked quietly into its ears. The three other lads stood watching, transfixed as the muscles on the big animal relaxed and the fear slipped from his eyes.

'He's a bloody horse whisperer,' one of the lads muttered.

'More like a witch doctor,' another one muttered even more quietly. There was humour in his comment. How ignorant they were, if only they knew.

Sam took the head collar lead and gently encouraged the horse to move forward with him. It did so willingly. As its front hooves touched the wooden ramp, there was some hesitation, but Sam was there, encouraging. No shoving, no swearing, just gentle persuasion. Step by step he walked him up the ramp and into the truck, where he secured him and gave the horse one last nose rub.

'All yours,' he said to the watching audience.

One of the grooms came out with a string of expletives.

'What did you say to him? I ain't never seen him get on a truck like that,' another one said.

Sam smiled.

They said nothing. Just watched. They knew the truth.

10

Harrison's dreams were dominated by wild horses in a windswept wilderness. At one point he'd been back in Wales, on the mountains. Alone and grieving. When he awoke in a strange bed, the feeling of unease took longer to disappear. He longed to clear his mind of bad images and hidden faces. He needed fresh air and nature, an antidote to the darkness.

After a quick breakfast, Harrison checked out and took his Harley to Fordham Woods. He wasn't expecting to be let inside the barn, he wanted to walk around the woods, to reconnect with nature and test his tracking skills, see what signs he could find. It was a skill that needed constant practice and reinforcement. A wood was a good place to lose yourself and no harm doing it around a crime scene—you never knew what you might find.

It turned out that the wood was only a small one, and there were too many people out for a Sunday stroll with their dogs and kids for Harrison's liking, but he managed to avoid them for two hours by leaving the paths. He wandered among the trees, studying the ground, the pattern of broken undergrowth, animal droppings and tracks. He followed a rat trail, its feet in parallel lines and a small drag mark between them showing where its tail followed on. There were also dog prints, zig zagging like a horse's through the undergrowth, and a male pheasant. Harrison took time to identify the latter, its toes wider apart than other perching birds, with smooth toes and a stand out middle toe, he judged it to be male by the mark left on the ground by his tail.

It was a wet valley woodland, with the River Snail, a teeny tiny cousin of the mighty Thames which flowed past his flat. There were plenty of alders growing in the waterlogged ground, and reeds rising from brown pools; descendants of those that would have been cut and used for thatching in generations past.

It wasn't hard to locate the barn. A small army of forensic vans gave it away, and a police vehicle recovery truck, was slowly winching a black Land

Rover onto its back. Not hard to guess that it must be Paul Lester's car on its way to be examined back at the police garage. Harrison didn't want to draw attention to himself, he didn't fancy having to explain to uniformed officers what he was doing creeping around a crime scene, especially as he was totally out of his jurisdiction and here only at the invite of one detective who was probably already no longer in charge. He used stealth to get as close as he could, checking for any potential evidence around the site. He saw nothing unusual.

Instead, Harrison disappeared among the trees. He found a hidden fox hole, spotted a sleeping owl, and saw signs that a small herd of deer had recently passed through. He skirted the edge of Fordham Abbey's grounds, picking up the faint scent of the Sake brewery. A recent modern addition which probably wouldn't have gone down too well with the monks of the ancient Fordham Priory which once stood on the site.

When he found himself well away from anyone else, he stood silent and still for half an hour, listening to nature around him, not just the bird calls, but the tiny rustles in the bushes. The chomping and crunching of a mouse eating some tasty morsel deep under its foliage hideaway. It wasn't the endless hills and wilderness of Wales, or the remoteness of the off-beaten tracks in the New

Forest, but it had made him feel better. The city hadn't wiped the childhood training from his mind. He could tune in and connect when he needed to.

Mid-morning he called DS James. A harassed voice responded.

'Sorry, Dr Lane, we've got the owner of the barn, Craig Matlock, about to arrive to help us with our enquiries. He's a former jockey and a friend of Paul's. Paul is in with the pathologist now, so I'm hoping for some news later this afternoon, and forensics are in the barn.'

'I'm going to head back into London,' Harrison informed him.

'OK, I'm being pulled off leading this anyway, as I'm sure you'd realise. DS Brian O'Neil is taking it on, at least temporarily, under the DCI's eye. He's not led on an investigation before either, but we're so short staffed. I'll get him to keep you informed.'

'OK.'

'And, Harrison, sorry for ruining your weekend, I appreciate you coming to help.'

HARRISON PLUGGED himself into Jack Savoretti and fired up his Harley. He wanted to be back in London before a new band of rain arrived from the west. The prospect of riding back along sodden motorway carriageways with the spray from lorries and driving rain, was not an appealing one. If he was honest, he also wanted to be in town for the phone call from Tanya. Just in case she needed him.

He would have liked to get into the barn, more to tie up that annoying loose end than anything else, but that would have to wait. Harrison wondered if he would ever set foot back in this area again. It was going to be interesting to see if the new SIO wanted further advice. He guessed that might depend on what they found at the barn. If he was right, then there should be something that would complicate the investigation.

Harrison pulled up outside his Docklands apartment as Jack Savoretti was singing *Only You*. It brought Tanya back to the forefront of his mind. Not that she'd been far from it.

He'd made it home in good time. The first splashes of rain were just hitting the surface of the Thames and bouncing off the railings that ran along the road outside his building.

He breathed a sigh of relief as he let himself into his apartment and the still silence enveloped him. He was lucky, his flat had been one of the first of the Docklands warehouse redevelopments in the early 1970s and so it was generous on space. A former tea and cargo warehouse, he had the whole top floor to call his own. Three bedrooms, two of which were en suite, plus a family sized bathroom. The living space was a large open-plan sitting, dining, and kitchen area with light wooden floors and a mix of brick and cream painted walls. The big windows in the sitting-room looked out over the Thames, and with the double glazing you could barely hear life outside.

The apartment had been owned by his grandfather, a former City worker who had the foresight to see the investment potential of the old warehouses which at that time were mostly derelict and unwanted. Harrison had never had it valued, but he knew that by now his grandfather's investment would have beaten even his wildest dreams. For Harrison, it was the perfect escape from London life, and he was eternally grateful for the inheritance.

He'd not had long to get to know his grandparents. By the time they realised he existed, his mother was dead, and his grandmother was suffering from terminal cancer. Those had been tough years. Emotional fissures scored into his core which silently reminded him to be careful of loving, because it always ended in loss.

Harrison grabbed a glass of water and headed into the shower to wash the road from his body and mind.

Being alone in his flat had its advantages. He enjoyed the quiet, and he began to relax after a busy weekend, but it also had its problems. He started checking his phone constantly to see if Tanya had texted or called and he'd missed it. It wasn't like him to phone watch and each time he did it he admonished himself, but he couldn't help it. Harrison made himself a late lunch and put a wash on. He contemplated going for a run, but decided not to, and then he couldn't contain himself anymore. He texted her.

Hi, back in town. Everything OK with you? He pressed send, and he waited.

Harrison waited five minutes. Ten. Twenty. Half an hour. He could feel himself getting anxious so he put on some Sacred Spirit music and lit his incense burner, hoping to calm the agitation he could feel building up. It helped a little, transporting him back to his former Arizona home as '*Yeah-Noha,*' filled the flat. Harrison tried a few minutes of meditation, but the relief it gave didn't last long, his mind battling the effort to relax.

He rang Tanya's number. In his ear, the phone rang, and rang, and rang. Then her voicemail cut in announcing that she was unable to answer and could he leave a message. He did as he was told.

'Tanya, it's Harrison. I'm back in London and… yeah. Let me know if you want to talk.'

He threw the phone down onto the sofa and paced up and down. Various scenarios flashed through his mind—none of them good. Of course, she could have been called in to work. That was more than likely. He'd give her another couple of hours and then if he still didn't hear anything, he'd swing by her flat and check on her.

Forty-five minutes later, he told himself that he needed some fresh milk and a few other supplies and needed to go out anyway, so he might as well go and check on her at the same time. He totally ignored the fact that there was a small supermarket just a few streets away he could walk to.

It was a less than fifteen-minute ride to Tanya's flat, and he reckoned he could do it in ten if it was a real emergency. She'd given him the address after they'd spoken before, just in case the stalker had appeared, and she'd needed him.

Tanya lived in the basement of a converted house in Islington, so she had her own entrance door. The street was a nice residential area. Three-storey brick town houses, with the ground floor painted white with pretty, arch-shaped windows. Black railed front gardens led straight to the door for the three flats above ground which shared an entrance, and on the left, some steps led down to Tanya's basement flat. There were mature trees dotted along her side of the road. It was a nice wide road too, with a decent sized pavement and room for parking bays along both sides. The other side of the street was slightly different. There was a pub at the end and running down from that a selection of what looked like offices which had once been small shops. Small alleyways split these up. Harrison would have to investigate later and see where these led. The most important thing was to check Tanya was OK.

He locked up his bike and headed down the steps to her flat. There was a light on in the window. He could just see that through the chinks in the blind, but otherwise, the blind was sealed shut. He found that a little strange at this time of the day. There was still plenty of daylight and living in a basement flat, he'd have thought she'd embrace the natural light of the sun, not shut it out.

Harrison knocked and waited. He could see that a new lock had recently been added. There was evidence of freshly gouged wood and paintwork. Above his head, a small camera was fixed, trained on the space in front of the door. Good, she'd done as she'd promised and put in some CCTV and stronger security.

Harrison knocked again and called out, 'Tanya, it's Harrison Lane.'

He had just got the words out when there was the sound of footsteps behind the door and it was flung open.

'Harrison!' Tanya exclaimed. 'Sorry I wasn't expecting anyone.'

'I tried calling but there was no reply. I just wanted to be sure you were OK. If now isn't good, it's not a problem.'

'No, no please come in, come in.' She waved him in quickly, peering around him at the street above. 'I'm really sorry. I broke my phone. Managed to drop it and totally smashed the screen. I haven't been able to send or receive any messages or phone calls.'

Harrison walked into a comfortable sitting-room area with a dining and kitchen space at the far end. There was a surprising amount of light, despite the closed blinds, but he wasn't looking at the flat, he was concentrating on Tanya who looked decidedly jittery.

'Has something happened?' he asked.

The fact she took too long to answer told him all he needed to know.

'Has he done something?'

Tanya turned away from him. Was he mistaken? Did she just not want him there? Then he saw her shoulders vibrate. He moved quickly around to face her, half turning her at the same time by placing his hands firmly on the top of her arms. She was trying to hold back tears.

'I'm sorry,' she whispered, 'I've just had a horrible weekend. He's really got to me and I don't know what to do.'

Harrison enveloped her in a hug, and they stood like that for what seemed like forever as she brought herself under control. Despite the circumstances, it felt good to hold her. She fitted perfectly in his arms and he put his cheek on her silky hair, drinking in her scent.

'Sorry, you're the first friend I've seen since…'

'Since what?' Harrison asked.

She gave a huge sigh that seemed to prompt her strength to return and walked over to the breakfast bar in her kitchen. A large roof window above them gave all the light he needed to see the anniversary card and silk underwear, which both sat in evidence bags on the top.

'This is a lot worse than you told me before,' Harrison said. He realised the energy in his voice that had come from concern, sounded a little angry.

'I know, it's got worse in the last few weeks. I'd hoped he'd get bored, but—'

'You should know people like this don't get bored. They just up their fantasies believing you're either going along with it, or they're enjoying scaring you. You can't ignore this and hope it will go away.'

Tanya nodded. 'I know.'

'Have you any idea who this could be? The likelihood is that it's someone who you've already had a relationship with. Only a very small minority of stalkers are complete strangers.'

She shook her head sadly.

'I honestly can't think of anyone. I know it's not Gary, my ex from last year. He's happily in another relationship and we still talk occasionally. We're friendly.'

'A neighbour?' Harrison asked, watching her face closely.

Tanya thought hard.

'I don't think so, but I just don't know.' Her face crumpled again, and she turned away from him.

'OK, the only way we're going to stop this is to identify him. Once we know who it is we can use the law and any other means we have, to get him to stop. He's no right to do this to you and make you feel this way.'

'I know and I feel so weak, but I'm paranoid that he can see into my flat somehow. I even tried to cover over the roof window yesterday, but I couldn't reach it.'

Harrison looked up. He could see nothing but sky through the big glass square above their heads. He couldn't even see how someone in the house above would be able to see in. The kitchen roof light wasn't a threat.

At the far end of the flat there were sliding patio doors into a tiny, paved garden. Harrison looked out, searching for any potential vantage points for someone to be able to peer in. Then he unlocked the doors and went outside.

'Who lives upstairs?' he asked. 'And on either side? Do you know them? Sit down and draw a diagram of everyone you know in the street, like a map. That way we can isolate any potentials or any residents you don't already know.'

Tanya nodded and set to it straight away. Instantly, she felt better. Harrison was helping her to regain control. This man was not going to beat her and make her scared in her own home.

Harrison went to the front of the flat now, street side. He opened the blinds, looking again at the potential eyeline and vantage points for someone to look in. He turned a lamp on in the sitting-room and put the TV on, then he rolled the blinds up fully and went outside. He stood in various places on the street outside. What he couldn't do was see what those on higher floors could see, but he had a good idea. Even with a height advantage, the position of the flat windows below street level afforded virtually no view of Tanya's flat. In fact, from what he could see, there was no position which would give a satisfying watching experience. The viewer might catch tiny glimpses, but certainly any voyeur wouldn't find it stimulating and satisfying.

Harrison looked at the blank windows up and down the street. Blind eyes stared back at him. Was there a predator behind one of them? Did they watch Tanya arriving and leaving her flat? Or was it someone else, perhaps at work, who is with her during the day and follows her home? There were certainly vantage points where they could hide in shadows and watch her house.

He returned to Tanya's flat, a thousand thoughts rushing through his head.

'Do you mind if I look in the bathroom and bedroom?' he asked.

Tanya looked up from what she was writing and shook her head. 'No, go ahead. Look at whatever you need to.'

The bathroom was small and windowless, definitely not a weak point. He pushed her bedroom door open and immediately felt like he was invading her privacy. It was a pretty room, feminine but practical, which fitted with her personality. It smelt of her perfume, and for a few moments, Harrison was distracted from what he should be doing. He gave himself a mental slap and focused on the one window in the room. It looked out onto a high wall, the retaining wall for the ground floor garden. There was no possibility of someone peeping in here. He crossed to the window to double check there was no hidden technology and cameras. There wasn't. He left quickly, mindful of not wanting to make her feel more vulnerable than she was already feeling.

When he got back to the kitchen, she was boiling the kettle while staring at the diagram and list of names she'd produced.

'Have you had any workmen in here in the last year?' he asked her.

She thought for a moment and then shook her head.

'No. Not for ages.'

'And you own the flat? There's no landlord with access?'

'I do and no. Nobody else has a key apart from my parents.'

That made him worry less that somebody could have come in and put hidden cameras in the flat. It was still a possibility, but he'd deal with that later.

'I think that's everyone I can think of,' she said to him as he approached.

'OK. I'll take a look through. But you need to report this, get those properly logged as evidence.' He nodded at the card and underwear.

'What kind of person is he?' she asked quietly. 'Is there a type of person who does this?'

'There's not one type,' said Harrison. 'I can't tell yet who we're dealing with because I need to know if it's someone who has an existing relationship with you, no matter how brief, or admires you from afar. There are many different motivations behind stalkers. I *am* concerned that he seems to be escalating his contact with you.'

Tanya nodded. 'I know, me too. I won't let him win, though. He's unnerved me this weekend, but I won't let him get to me like this again.'

Harrison smiled weakly at her. He hadn't been totally honest, just the items the stalker had already sent to Tanya had given him a good idea of what kind of person they were dealing with, but if he'd told her the full truth, that would have scared her even more.

11

Harrison had reluctantly left Tanya alone. He'd not wanted to offer to stay because that seemed presumptuous, and he hadn't asked if she'd wanted to come home with him for the same reasons. Besides, he knew what she'd say to that one. Tanya was a strong woman who wouldn't want to be chased out of her home. He did make her promise to get a new mobile phone asap and if she had any concerns to call him immediately. When he left, though, it was with a sense of unease. She'd promised to get the card and underwear into the lab and report what was going on, but he too didn't hold out too much hope of them throwing a light on their sender.

He didn't sleep well. It wasn't wild horses that chased through his dreams, but dark shadows that were just out of reach. By the time he woke up, he'd decided what he was going to do about the stalker, although he wouldn't share his plan with Tanya just yet.

There'd been no more communications from DS James or anyone else in Cambridge, and so he'd gone into his office to see what new cases needed his help. Harrison's work bolt-hole was in the basement of New Scotland Yard, the Metropolitan Police headquarters. The building was actually on Victoria Embankment, but still carried the historic name of the original headquarters, which once had its public entrance on Great Scotland Yard.

Harrison's office wasn't like most other people's workspaces. The average office was a sterile characterless place in which to sit and get on with your job. His served the same function, but in a more distinctive way. As the lights flickered on, he was met by a wall of occult artefacts, voodoo dolls, staring empty-socketed death masks, Ouija boards, and animal skulls, jammed in between ancient books on the dark arts, folklore, and every religion you could think of, plus more. On the left was a neat desk with a computer screen and pinboard, to the right another desk with two screens and piles of clutter, most of it junk food packets and soft drinks.

Ryan, his technical assistant, would be arriving soon.

What Harrison did immediately notice was the mug sat on his own desk. It still carried the remains of last week's herbal tea. Ryan's bin was also more than half filled. He sighed. This week's cleaner had obviously been one of the more superstitious in the workforce. It was potluck each morning to find out if they'd been brave enough to venture into the office, or had instead refused to cross the threshold, signing the cross and praying for deliverance. He couldn't be angry. He understood the strength of faith and beliefs more than anyone, but it was an irritation.

Most of the artefacts were items he'd collected from cases over the years. All of them solved, all of them proven to be the controlling nature of evil human behaviour and not some dark force. He'd tried to talk to the cleaners once, explained the nature and background to his mementos, but the turnover of staff, and the dark, lonely basement, had proved to be a worthy opponent and he'd given up. This had been the first time for a while that the cleaning hadn't been done.

What Harrison didn't know was that his office had become the initiation rite for all new cleaning team members. The rest of the staff would keep quiet and let the unsuspecting newbie go into the office, then watch their reaction. It had slightly backfired last night as it had taken the supervisor half an hour to calm down his Nigerian born new recruit, who'd walked in without putting the lights on and come face to face with a particularly evil looking voodoo doll in the semi-darkness.

On Harrison's desk was a printout of a dark watercolour in what looked like an old notebook. He didn't need to read the note that came with it to know where it was. It showed what looked like a hill in the country. At the top of the hill were two tall trees, and in the distance, past miles of fields and pathways, was the dome of St Paul's Cathedral. This was a view from Nunhead Hill, which was now the site of Nunhead Cemetery. Harrison would also bet that at least one of the tall oak trees pictured was the one he had stood under recently. The one that sheltered his nightmares, the dark secret of a murder he'd witnessed as a child.

Ryan had scribbled him a note, *Found this. Didn't have GPS in those days but reckon it's just across from the location you gave me. If you were standing on the top of the hill where the trees are, that would give you the same eyeline to St Paul's. It's by JMW Turner 1796-97. Just over forty years before the cemetery was built there.*

Harrison sat down. It didn't give him any more clues as to why that location should have been used for a Satanic ritual, but hills overlooking, and away from cities, were often the sites of witch hangings and the like. Ryan had been searching for a while and found nothing. Seeing as the Internet didn't exist back then, it was hard having to find scant physical records, and that was if it had even been official. While Janet Horne had been the last person in the UK to be executed legally for witchcraft in 1727, she certainly wasn't the last to die because of it. Harrison knew that his best bet was going to be to investigate the most recent murder, that of an unknown woman in 1993. She'd been stabbed and killed in some kind of Satanic ritual. There had been plenty of witnesses, Harrison knew that because he and his mother had been two of them. After that, his mother had taken them out of the country to America, only to return years later to be murdered herself.

Ryan was trying to find out if there were any other witnesses, but so far, they all seemed to have disappeared into the ether, like spirits in the graveyard. It was another fleck of a clue, but one which wouldn't advance his hunt for his mother's killers. He stuck the Turner painting on his pinboard, next to the newspaper cutting about the Nunhead murder, and the photograph of three people, two women flanking a man with a black cloak. One of the women was a pretty blond, his mother, gazing adoringly at the man. The other was a hard-faced woman staring straight at the camera. He knew the pair were out there, they'd taken the trouble of becoming reacquainted with him recently. He just had to find them and bring them to justice, but for that, he might need some help.

'Here he is. Merlin's back in the building.' DS Jack Salter's cheeky smiling face was the one Harrison had come to see. He was sitting in the middle of the Major Investigation Team's incident room on the second floor of Lewisham Police Station. Busy detectives and their support staff occupied half the other desks around him. The rest were empty, their occupants out interviewing and visiting crime scenes. Just a normal day. Harrison's arrival always caused a little stir of interest, several of the women's eyes were drawn away from their computer screens to appraise him, and those who hadn't worked with him before, but heard about his reputation, looked to see the man in the flesh. There'd been a few nods of hello from those who'd been on Operation Genesis with him. Respect was the definite vibe in the room, but those who knew him also understood that stopping for a chat wasn't his thing.

'Jack,' was all Harrison replied, nodding. He didn't take offence at the jibes; he knew it was Jack's way.

Jack wasn't a small build. Even in his thirties, he carried on playing rugby and was fit, standing at six foot one, but when Harrison perched on the edge of his desk, he managed to make him somehow look average. Jack looked a lot better than the last time he'd seen him. Then his hands had been bandaged from the cuts and burns they'd received while trying to rescue a kidnapped boy. He was still looking tired, though. 'How's Marie?' he asked, and watched as the smile weakened and the twinkle left Jack's eyes.

'Fine. Daniel's sleeping five hours a night now, so we're getting some more sleep. A couple of whiskies in his milk every night has been working a treat.'

Typical of Jack, always hated being too serious for long. Harrison knew how devoted he was to his family, and how he also found it hard to talk about his wife's postnatal depression. It had been a huge worry and taken its toll on them all. Harrison didn't push the subject, a busy incident room wasn't the best place for a private conversation, but he'd seen Jack's eyes wander to the small photograph of Marie and Daniel that was stuck to his screen and knew that things were definitely not yet 'fine'.

'Good weekend?' Jack asked.

'Cambridgeshire asked for some assistance on a case.'

'You get around a bit now. Whereabouts? Marie's parents live to the east of Cambridge.'

'Around Newmarket. Victim was a jockey.'

'That's just down the road from them. Not Paul Lester, was it? Saw that on the news this morning. Hadn't realised there'd been any funny business with it.'

Funny business was Jack's way of meaning a ritualistic crime. The fact it hadn't been reported as such was good news for the investigating team, and obviously they'd confirmed the victim's ID too. Things were progressing.

DCI Sandra Barker interrupted their conversation as she came out of her office and spotted Harrison in among her team.

'Harrison!' she exclaimed with a big smile on her face. 'I hope you were coming to say hello to me?'

Harrison smiled. One of his rare, full face smiles that not only curved his mouth, but lit up his eyes and wrapped the recipient in warmth. Sandra Barker was immune to his manly charms, quite content with her husband, too tired to have an affair, and anyway, too old for Harrison; but she could fully appreciate the attraction. Theirs was more of a mother/son relationship. She liked him, they'd been working together for a few years now and had gradually built a close bond. Above all, she knew she could trust him. At first, Sandra had been one of only a handful of senior officers to try out the maverick 'witch hunter' in the new Ritualistic Behavioural Crime unit. As soon as she'd witnessed him on a case, and most importantly the impact he had on results, using his services had become a no brainer. She'd helped him too, giving advice on the way things worked at the Met, so his career had flourished and not ended in drama. Now his reputation had spread, not just through the Met, but across the UK forces.

'I've had Leo Fawcett from the National Crime Agency, on the phone about you,' she said to him.

Harrison didn't register anything on his face. He wasn't a man easily impressed or stressed.

'They're wondering why you're just working under the Met badge, he's after you for nationwide support.'

Harrison nodded. 'I already help out where I can,' he said.

'I know, but it's quite possible that the more you get pulled out of London, the more questions will get asked about budget here. Could give you the chance to get out the city though, we know how much you love the lifestyle!' Sandra smiled at him knowing full well he'd understand she was being sarcastic, 'Just so you're aware. They might approach you direct soon.'

Harrison nodded.

'Don't forget us in Lewisham,' Jack added. He might have started off as a complete sceptic about Harrison's reputation, but after Operation Genesis, he knew it was well deserved. He'd even come to like Harrison Lane. The guy had virtually carried him out of a burning building to safety and went above and beyond to find the missing boy. In Jack's books, he was genuine, a good bloke.

'I've been trying to persuade DI Salter here to have a break for a week or so, spend some time away with Marie and Daniel,' DCI Barker said pointedly to Jack. She'd been worried about him and the toll that Marie's mental health was having on Jack's.

'That's an excellent idea,' Harrison replied. 'Different surroundings are a good way to reset the brain. For Marie, depression makes it more difficult to alter behaviours, she's not got the motivation. She needs support to make the changes, and that can come from those around her and the environment. She would also benefit from spending more time outdoors in a natural setting. Nature is good for helping you reconnect, and you're more likely to get that out of London.'

'OK, doc,' Jack replied, slightly sarcastically, but there was no malevolence in his tone.

Harrison raised his eyebrows at him, and Jack realised he didn't know if he was joking or not.

'Thanks for the advice, I'll see if I can persuade Marie to come away with me for a long weekend. It's not been easy persuading her to leave the house to go to the supermarket lately, let alone get out of town.'

'Try with somewhere she's familiar with,' Harrison advised.

'Well, I'd better get back to work,' DCI Barker said. 'I'm currently the queen of multi-tasking. Got two cases about to hit the courts, two ongoing, and another that Interpol is helping us with. I feel like a circus juggler.'

'You know that there's no such thing as multi-tasking.' Harrison turned to Sandra now. 'You physically can't do more than one thing at once. Your brain isn't capable of it because it can only process one set of information at a time. It just has to switch its attention. It's not an effective way to work because you're taking up brain power to switch and refocus. You're better off focusing on one thing at once. It's more efficient and less tiring.'

Sandra wasn't sure how to respond.

'OK, thanks, Harrison. I'll bear that in mind. Good to see you and I'd better get back to focusing on one of my cases.' She smiled and headed back to her office, where she promptly rewarded herself with a chocolate for having defied biology and psychiatry and managed to multi-task for most of her career.

'So, what brings you to Lewisham?' Jack asked Harrison.

'Actually, I have a couple of favours to ask,' Harrison replied.

That hadn't been something Jack expected.

12

Harrison returned to his bolt-hole, where Ryan was busy checking out Tanya's neighbours and the rest of the list she'd compiled.

'Anything flagging up?' Harrison asked him.

Ryan shook his head.

'A couple of random eccentrics, one guy who has one of the world's largest collections of airline sick bags, although believe it or not, it's not the largest. He's got just over four thousand! *Guinness Book of Records* said the largest collection is over six thousand. What possesses someone to collect barf bags? What can you possibly get out of having thousands of them? Apart from a puking fetish, that seems to be his only vice. He works for London Transport.'

'Could be how he gets around while stalking?'

'Maybe, but there's nothing to suggest he's our man. The only other eccentric is a woman who has had all her pet cats stuffed. She's up to about a dozen now, and she has them all in her sitting-room. How freaky must that be, walking into a room with a dozen glass-eyed dead cats all staring at you? Most of the rest of them round there are young professionals, very few of the flats are single occupancy.'

'And the offices across the road?' Harrison asked.

'Just working on those now. Proving slightly tougher, but again, no red flags yet although if he's a first-time stalker, there might be nothing unusual to flag up.'

Harrison sighed, but had already suspected it wasn't going to be simple. Jack had also not come up with anything for that neighbourhood. For the first of Harrison's requested favours, he'd run the street through the registered sex offenders list. If it was a neighbour who was stalking Tanya, they didn't have a record. The field was still open. Too far open for his liking. Time for Plan B.

First things first. He checked his emails. There was one from DI Chowdhury, who'd made some arrests after he'd helped her with a sickening case of modern slavery using Brazilian Jurema and Macumba cult practices. They had a trial date, and she was warning him they'd need him in court to testify. She also asked for any book recommendations so that she could read up on the religion. Harrison enquired after the young woman they'd found alive and sent her a couple of book suggestions.

He'd just managed to get through his email backlog when one popped into his inbox from DCI Whittaker in Cambridgeshire. It was the pathologist's report. Harrison opened the document and read how Paul Lester had met his death. It gave him even more reason to think they were missing something. Paul's neck showed signs of prior manual strangulation. Somebody had tried to choke him to death with their hands. It hadn't been what killed him, that had been the hangman's noose, but it would have been sufficient to have incapacitated him. As Harrison suspected, they cut his heart out just after death.

The DCI told him that the barn was a smorgasbord of fingerprints and DNA, and they were trying to track down who might have been there over the past weeks. Craig Matlock wasn't being overly forthcoming and so they were keeping him in custody for as long as they were allowed. The Horsemen were their prime suspects after various bizarre ritual items had been found. One was a stick which DCI Whittaker attached a photograph of in the email. It was a cane, but on the top was a pair of horns, and on the bottom, what looked to be the hoof from a goat. Another photograph was of a horse's skull, placed in a cavity within the barn. None of these items surprised Harrison. He wrote back to tell the DCI that the stick was almost certainly ceremonial, that they would have used it in meetings to swear their oaths, possibly also as an object to hold during meetings to show that the person with it, was the one who should be speaking within the circle. The horse skull was quite common in barns of that age, often buried within walls or roof spaces, or under floors, to protect the building from evil spirits. Cats and shoes were often found in the walls of houses for the same reason. Harrison also flagged up the pathologist's report and suggested that two people could have been involved, although only one of them went with Paul to the Fen. He knew this would strengthen the DCI's belief that it was the Horsemen who were behind the killing, but there was something not quite straightforward with the case. He'd need to speak to Craig before he could make any further judgements. He asked the DCI if he was going to need his further advice and if he wanted him to be present for interviews. Harrison didn't like to leave a case when it was clearly nowhere near to being solved. He was sure the barn would hold further clues, as long as you knew what you were looking for.

'You want anything from the canteen boss?' Ryan asked him, breaking through his thoughts.

'No thanks, Ryan,' he replied.

'Of course, it's Monday, one of your fasting days. I'm just going to grab a hot chocolate.'

'I'll probably be gone before you get back, so take your key.'

'Always have it on me.' Ryan smiled at his boss. He knew Harrison well enough to know that he could be there one moment and gone the next.

Harrison completed the online transaction he had opened and shut down his computer. Time for Tanya Plan B.

IT HAD TAKEN him a while to find exactly the right vehicle. Harrison needed something that afforded as much of an all-round view as possible, but also had tinted windows. He wanted to look out; he didn't want anyone seeing in. Tanya said she felt like the man was watching her when she returned home. If she was right, Harrison intended to make sure he saw exactly who it was. He left his Harley at home and took the rented van to Tanya's street. He'd needed to drive around for a while before the ideal parking space became available. The staff in the little offices opposite were leaving for the day, and he managed to bag a spot before another resident came home.

Watching down the street both ways and keeping his eyes on the windows, as well as street level, was not going to be easy on his own. Harrison borrowed three surveillance cameras from work and set them up to watch the street from various angles. That way, he could watch them after and make sure he hadn't missed something. Or, if he was lucky, and the stalker showed his face, they'd have him on camera.

Harrison had purposely not told Tanya he was going to be there. If she knew, then she might give him away accidentally. Even the subtlest difference in her behaviour could alert the man that something was going on. Harrison had dressed for speed. He'd left his bike leathers at home and had on a pair of joggers with trainers and a hoody. He wasn't keen on being identified, either. This was a long way from being official police business and if word got back to the Met, he knew it wouldn't look good for him. It was a risk he was prepared to take, though. He would not sit by and let Tanya become scared to live her life. Worst still, he feared this man was building up to launch some kind of attack on her. He was escalating, and the gifts were becoming sexual. This wasn't an innocent crush.

At just before 6 p.m., Tanya turned the corner of the road and started walking towards her flat. She'd told Harrison that she took the Tube so he'd been expecting her to come from that direction. Just the way she walked made his blood boil. She was clearly anxious. Her gait was stiff and precise. Her eyes kept shifting from side to side and all around. Whoever was doing this to her had to be stopped.

Although Harrison wanted to watch Tanya, he had to tear his eyes away from her and look around the street. What curtains moved? What shadows appeared? Was someone watching from one of the alleyways down between the offices?

He watched. Tanya walked down the steps to her flat, but she hesitated before putting the key in the lock and going in. From Harrison's street level vantage point, he couldn't see what she'd bent her head to look at, but she paused, gave a quick look around and plunged the key into the door without bending down to whatever the object was. Harrison wondered if there had been another delivery. If there had, then there was a very strong chance the man was watching to see her reaction. He saw the lights go on through the chinks in the blind. He scanned the street. There was nobody else in sight. No curtains twitched, no glint of a camera lens in the light, no figures following her down the street. Perhaps he wasn't here tonight, after all.

Tanya's door opened again and her shape, silhouetted by the light behind her, appeared. She made it obvious that she had gloves on, and in her hand was an evidence bag. She bent down and scooped something into the bag before sealing it. Tanya stood there defiantly, a clear message to whoever might have sent the package that she wasn't intimidated, and she was going to take the item in for examination and report it.

Harrison gave a smile to himself, she was a tough woman, but he had to focus on the street and not on admiring her. The man had to be there somewhere, watching. He'd want to see the effect his *gift* had on its target.

Harrison still saw nothing.

Tanya dropped the gift onto the floor of her hall and shut the door on the street. The show was over. Where was the VIP audience of one?

Then he saw it. Only a tiny movement, but Harrison was out of the van and heading straight for the alleyway opposite Tanya's flat within seconds.

13

Harrison hurtled down the street to the entrance of the alleyway where he'd seen a shadow withdraw. He arrived just in time to see someone disappear from the other end of the dark alley and turn left. The passageway was narrow, so running full pelt down it when you were Harrison's bulk, took some precision. He banged his elbow as he reached the end and burst back into the light, where he found himself on a dirt path that ran the full length of the street. There were the small offices and houses on one side and a thin strip of waste ground on the other.

Harrison saw the man in front of him stop and turn to look at what the noise was behind him. There was a moment's hesitation as six foot two of muscle started running straight at him.

The moment was so brief, Harrison almost missed it, as a mask of calm settled on the man's features. He made no move to run, just stepped back from the path.

Harrison had literally three seconds in which to make a decision. He could confront the man and risk sending him underground and perhaps making him more dangerous, or he could play it smart. At the moment, the man had no idea if Harrison was coming for him, but he was prepared to bluff it. A thin, less than six-foot man with thinning black hair and a beak of a nose, like some weird crow-like bird, was standing his ground as a six-foot two threat came at him full pelt. That took some courage. Or it took the unemotional bluffing capabilities of a sociopath. Harrison's psychology training kicked in and overrode his primitive desire to just shove him up against the wall and thump him.

'Do you know how I get to the Tube from here? I'm late, going to miss my train at Waterloo. Map said this was a short cut?' Harrison held up his phone and peered at it like he was viewing a map.

The man looked at him impassively.

'Turn right at the end,' he said. It was a Scottish accent carried by a thin and reedy voice.

'Cheers,' Harrison replied, and ran on past him. He had what he needed.

Harrison followed the instructions and as soon as he could, dived into a café along the street and waited to see if the man walked past. He did. Harrison watched as calmly and purposefully he strode past, head bobbing forward with each step. Back straight. Dead eyes fixed forward. The man headed down the steps that led to the Tube station.

Harrison could be wrong. The man might just have been walking down the alley from one of the offices, heading towards the Underground, but he didn't think so. There was something cold and unnerving about the passive face which now stared back at him from his mobile phone. Harrison hoped the guy hadn't clocked him taking his photograph when he'd been pretending to look at the map. It was possible that he'd been watching over the weekend and had seen him come to Tanya's flat. If he had, then he was even more of a cool customer than he thought.

What he did now know for sure was that this wasn't some love-struck groupie desperate to win Tanya's affections. This man was cold and calculating. There was no passion to what he did, just emotional and mental torture. What was he capable of? Most importantly, who was he?

Harrison retraced his steps, looking at the ground in the alleyway for signs that the man had been there watching. He found a patch of ground that was devoid of any rubbish or dirt. Somebody had been standing there for quite some time, and their feet had gradually cleared the debris from the spot. He'd noticed a small patch of green on the upper arm of the man's coat, and the wall of the alley was layered in a thin coating of lichen. There were several small patches where the lichen had been brushed from the wall. Someone had lent against it, and not just once or twice.

Harrison was convinced he was their man. Question was, did Tanya know him? Could she identify him? There was only one way of finding that out.

He could hear music playing in the flat when he rang Tanya's doorbell. Loud, upbeat pop. Clearly a distraction technique to get her into a positive mood after her unnerving return home. It was immediately turned off and there was a silence after he'd rung. He could imagine her rushing over to the CCTV feed and looking to see who it was at her door. Moments later it was opened.

'Harrison.' Tanya smiled at him. 'You're making a habit of surprising me.'

Immediately, he felt guilty.

'I'm sorry,' he said, not stepping into the flat. 'I just wanted to show you something it won't take a moment.'

'Don't be silly. I'm so pleased you're here. Come in.' Tanya waved him in and did her usual quick check of the street as she closed the door behind him. He glanced at the small, flat box that was on the floor of the hall inside the evidence bag. There was no identifying branding on it. It wouldn't be flowers then. There was a certain type of company that didn't brand their boxes so as not to embarrass recipients. It was clear Tanya had no intention of opening it in her home.

'I may have a photograph of the man who is watching you, but you must understand that I'm not 100 percent sure that it's him.' Even as he said it, he knew that wasn't true. Talking to him, watching him walk past, checking out the alley, all of it had convinced him he was right and that man was Tanya's stalker.

'How did you get it?' Tanya started.

'I was parked outside in a van when you came home,' Harrison said, realising as he said it that it sounded like he was being a stalker.

Tanya's face turned into a frown.

'Outside?'

'Yes. I want you to know who's doing this. If we can identify him, then we can deal with him.'

She took a few steps away from Harrison and sat down on the sofa.

'Why didn't you tell me?'

'If I'd told you, you might have given me away. I needed you to be acting exactly as you usually would.'

'I was the bait,' she said quietly.

'No,' he replied forcefully this time. 'I was there to protect you. I want to help. I'm concerned that this man might become dangerous.'

Tanya looked up at his face and he saw the fear in her eyes and instantly felt guilty for putting it there. Then he checked himself. It wasn't him doing this to her, it was the man. He took his phone from his pocket and found the photograph.

'Do you recognise this man?'

Tanya gave a small gasp, and Harrison saw her body tense.

'Yes. His girlfriend was murdered. I don't think anyone was ever charged. I remember him because he gave me the creeps. When we were at her house, he would turn up outside watching, like some crow out of that Hitchcock *Birds* movie. My colleague Dave said it was just because he was so upset about her murder.'

'When was this?' Harrison asked.

'About a year ago now. The last time I saw

him was at the inquest when the body was released. There was no other family. I think he claimed her.'

There was silence for a moment. A huge screaming siren of a silence while they both thought about what she'd just said.

'Do you think he's just trying to replace her and because I was there has latched on to me?' she asked Harrison. 'Or maybe he blames us, me, for not getting a conviction? Or…' Tanya didn't finish her sentence.

He nodded slowly.

'I think we have to consider the possibility he might have been watching you all investigate his own handiwork. We need to get in touch with the SIO on that case, and you need to find yourself somewhere else to live for a while. You can't stay here on your own. I don't think he clocked me, but if he did he might speed up his game plan.'

14

Harrison had every intention of returning to his apartment alone, but the friend Tanya wanted to go and stay with was out at her boyfriend's parents' house for dinner. There was no way he was going to let her stay at home alone and so they'd agreed that she'd come back to his for the night while the man wasn't there to see her take things out, and then he'd help her move to the friend's tomorrow.

While having Tanya in the flat seemed like a pleasant idea, it was also an extremely uncomfortable prospect. He'd not lived with anyone for over a decade, and this was his refuge. A place he could totally relax. He'd had no one over to visit before, apart from Joe when he'd come to the UK and stayed with him for a week.

That had been totally different. Joe was family. He may have only been his stepfather, but he'd been the best influence in his young life. Not only did he teach him tracking, but he'd stabilised his mother. Those had been their happiest years, staying with the Tohono O'odham people in Arizona. Later, after his mother's murder, Joe had saved his life. He was always a welcome guest.

The reason Harrison told himself that he didn't want Tanya staying was because he would be more use to her if he could go back tomorrow and see if the Scottish sociopath had returned. Tanya would be safe at her friend's house on the other side of town. He also knew there were other reasons, but those he chose to ignore.

As it was, he helped her pack and set up some automated lights to make it look like she was still inside. For now, she would be OK. Tomorrow, or the next day, the man would work out that she'd moved elsewhere. He knew where she worked. It was just going to be a question of time before he followed her to the friend's house. They had to act quickly.

The van had come in useful for transporting her and the few bags she had to safety. Harrison made absolutely sure that they weren't followed or watched.

Sitting in the confines of the van, so close together, Harrison could almost smell her fear.

'What makes you think he's dangerous?' she'd asked him. They'd stopped at a traffic light and neither of them had spoken for a while. Her voice, quiet and fragile, shattered the air in the van. He wanted to be honest with her, but he also didn't want to frighten her unnecessarily.

'I'm a grown woman who works in crime. I've seen more death and violence than 95 percent of the population. You can tell me,' she said as though she could read his thought process.

'He didn't run,' Harrison said to her, his eyes quickly glancing her way before returning to the road ahead as the lights turned green.

'Didn't run?'

'I ran after him, and he didn't run. He just turned round to face me calmly. People don't usually do that. If they're guilty, they'll run too, if they're not then they're going to be scared by a big stranger running straight at them. He was neither.'

'What does that mean?' she asked him. 'Maybe he just didn't think he had anything to worry about.' He could feel her eyes on his face, watching for any signs that he wasn't being honest.

'It means he doesn't consider his own safety, he has no feelings of guilt, and he thinks he's clever enough to be able to get himself out of any situation.'

'A sociopath.' Tanya finished Harrison's diagnosis for him.

'I think so,' he said.

'It doesn't mean he killed his girlfriend, though,' she replied. 'Not all sociopaths are killers.'

'No, you're right. There are some very successful businesspeople and politicians who are sociopaths. The ruthless trait can be quite useful. So why is he watching your flat and sending you gifts? He's playing with you. What we don't know is what his end game is.'

That had the effect of killing the conversation.

He tried not to look at her while he was driving, but he could tell she was biting her lip to keep back the tears. Harrison felt awful for upsetting her, but at the same time he needed Tanya to realise how serious the situation could be. He'd looked in the man's eyes. They were cold and dark, like a shark's. Whatever he was up to, it wasn't good. People like that scared him far more than any folklore or Satanic stories. There was something wrong with the souls of people like him. An empty, cold grey shadow filled his insides, not the warm rainbow kaleidoscope of normal human beings.

. . .

Despite the circumstances, Tanya was looking forward to seeing the inner sanctum of Dr Harrison Lane. He was such an enigma that she couldn't imagine what kind of home he'd made for himself. Ever since meeting him, she'd conjured up a range of possibilities, from a warm country cottage feel to a sterile steel and pale oak bachelor pad. Was he tidy, or would it be cluttered with all manner of oddities, like his office? She hadn't even known for sure if he lived alone, but if all the gossip was true, then he did.

'Wow,' was her reaction when Harrison opened the large internal front door to his flat, and she momentarily forgot about why she was there. A huge light-filled room was in front of her, with large windows all down one side, looking out over the Thames. A modern, open galley-style kitchen was at the far end, with a comfortable sitting area in front of it. The floors were all wooden, and the brick and white walls carried large photographs and a few artefacts of Native American people. Other than some simple furniture, the flat was sparsely decorated.

'You're not one for clutter, are you?' She smiled at Harrison.

'I don't need much.' He shrugged. 'Things end up owning you if you're not careful.'

'I should have gone into psychology,' Tanya continued, still looking around her. 'This place is amazing.'

'I inherited it,' Harrison said. He might not know how much it was worth, but he knew he wouldn't be able to afford to buy it now on his wages. 'You can have this room. It has an en suite.' He'd crossed the big open living expanse and opened a door at the start of a short corridor that obviously led to the bedrooms.

Tanya walked into a room which was as big as her sitting-room and kitchen combined, let alone her bedroom.

'I'll get some sheets,' Harrison said to her as her eyes flitted to the double bed. It looked new. The duvet was rolled up into a large fat sausage and there were four pristine pillows waiting for their case coverings.

'Thank you so much for doing this,' she said, turning to look at him. This was the first time the pair of them had stopped and properly looked at each other since the night they'd met in the wine bar. The stillness of the flat was like a vise pushing them together. Tanya felt the overwhelming urge to reach out and touch him. To let her hands run over his muscular arms, to feel the slightly rough stubble of his cheek on hers as she pushed her body against his solid chest. She needed comfort and safety, and he offered both. The flat smelt of him, the musky scent of the androstenone that made her pheromones race and her heart start to beat faster. His eyes didn't leave hers, she felt him drinking her in. For the first time, she was sure he wanted her too.

'I'll go ring for pizza. You must be hungry,' he said, turning quickly and leaving the room.

15

Harrison woke up early and had the desperate urge to go for a run. It was 5 a.m. and Tanya was still asleep. She was safe. The Scottish sociopath couldn't get her here. He'd written a note for her just in case she'd woken up, and then quietly let himself out of the flat.

He knew why he needed to run. Last night he'd very nearly given in to the need he had inside to touch her, hold her, make love to her. It had taken all his resolve to walk away and then spend the rest of the evening in her company. Quite apart from the fact he didn't want to get involved with anyone, it would have been taking advantage of the situation. She was vulnerable, scared, and if he'd opened his arms, he knew she would have sought their protection.

Running along the Thames at this time of the morning was a joy. A low mist had settled over the river and although the traffic hum was still there, it wasn't as loud and obtrusive as usual. Harrison ran, focusing on the sound of the air being pushed in and out of his lungs. The rhythmic thump of his feet on the pavement. For a few blissful moments, his mind was totally taken up with the exertion of exercise. Then the face of Tanya's stalker reappeared inside his head. He turned and ran back to the apartment, keen to get in and showered before she awoke. There was a lot of work to be done today.

A GENTLE KNOCKING sound woke Tanya. For a moment she wasn't sure where she was, and then it had all come flooding back to her.

'Come in,' she'd said after quickly raking her fingers through her hair.

Harrison pushed the door open with his foot, carrying a tray in his hands. He smiled warmly at her. There it was again, that look he gave her, the one which made her think he did like her. She'd seen it last night. She was convinced he had wanted her in that moment as much as she had him. As the evening went on, there was no further evidence of that attraction, and she'd come to doubt herself. He almost seemed to resent her for being there.

'I made breakfast. I hope you like scrambled eggs and bacon,' he said to her.

'Oh my goodness, you didn't have to. Thank you.'

He put the tray down on the bedside table and helped her to plump up the pillows behind her so she could sit up. Then he handed it to her. This was a gentle, caring side she'd never seen before.

'Are you not having any?' she asked.

'I've eaten. I went for a run earlier,' he replied. 'We need to talk about what you're going to do about the stalker today, and if you need my help.'

Tanya cut a slice of toast and scrambled egg and watched as Harrison sat on the armchair next to the bed. She could see the colour in his cheeks from the run, and his hair was still slightly damp from the shower, his skin freshly shaved.

'I'll get in touch with the SIO from the girlfriend's murder case first thing,' she said to him.

'Do you get on with him? Trust him?' he asked her.

'He's OK. I trust him yeah, but we're not best buddies.'

'Maybe we should report this to one of the MITs you know well. Someone who will understand that this is serious, and you wouldn't make a fuss if it wasn't.'

'But who?' Tanya asked, taking a bite of her breakfast. She couldn't quite believe she was sitting in bed eating a breakfast cooked by the very eligible Dr Harrison Lane, and that thought was distracting her.

For a moment, they were both silent. Harrison had bent forward, elbows on his knees, thinking.

She took a sip of the orange juice he'd placed on the tray for her.

'Leave it with me,' he said at last, and got up from the chair to head out the room. 'I'm afraid I only have herbal teas, no coffee. Would you like one?'

Tanya smiled and shook her head, her mouth full of breakfast.

'When you're ready, I'll give you a ride into work. We can come back later and pick up the van and your things.'

Then he was gone again, and she was left alone to finish her plate of breakfast.

HARRISON HAD JUST MADE himself a tea and heard the shower turn on in the spare room when his mobile phone rang. He put the mug on the counter and looked to see who it was. There was no name.

'Harrison Lane,' he answered.

'Dr Lane. I'm so sorry to call you this early. It's DCI Robert Whittaker. Do you have a moment to talk?'

'Sure.' Harrison picked up his tea and took it over to his sofa, where he could sit, staring out the windows as he talked.

The man on the other end of the phone sighed.

'We don't have anyone in custody yet, but we do have several strong leads, which we're working on today. Trouble is, I'm struggling with manpower here. We simply don't have the expertise to deal with this case right now. Our usual team has been decimated by illness, maternity leave, and case workload. As you know, DS James was due to lead the investigation but now can't and DS O'Neil is, well he's not got much experience.'

There was silence. DCI Whittaker waited for a reaction from Harrison. There was nothing.

'Dr Lane?'

'Yes, I'm listening.'

'OK, right, so I was calling to see if there is any possibility that you could head back up to give us the benefit of your expertise, just for this week.

It will help tremendously with interviewing our suspects. You know what you're looking for. We also need a good DS or DI to come in and assist with the interviews. We were going to go through the usual channels to request some additional resources, but I wondered if there was someone you might prefer to work with?'

Harrison's heart had plunged at the DCI's words. They weren't altogether unexpected, but right now was not the ideal time for him to be leaving London. Tanya needed him.

'I have something I need to take care of here,' he started.

'I appreciate you must be really busy, but I wouldn't ask unless I thought you could make a big difference.' The DCI was pleading now.

'I'll have to get back to you,' Harrison replied, and the DCI let out a big breath of relief at his words.

Harrison had already decided exactly who he was going to speak to about Tanya's problem, and now the DCI had asked this, he realised he was going to be seeing DCI Sandra Barker, with two requests.

16

DCI Sandra Barker's face lit up when the bulk of Harrison Lane filled her office doorway.

'Harrison!' she exclaimed. 'Two days in a row, we are honoured.'

Harrison closed the door behind him and turned back to see the DCI's face looking altogether more serious. Everyone knew that her door only got shut if you had something private and sensitive to discuss.

'Everything all right?' she asked, reaching into the top drawer of her desk for a chocolate. It was a natural distraction technique for when situations became tense. She knew she didn't need to bother offering Harrison one. He didn't eat chocolate. Much to her horror.

'Yes and no,' he replied.

DCI Barker waited.

'First, I wanted to talk to you about Dr Tanya Jones, she was the forensic lead on the Darren Phillips case.'

'Yes, of course. I've worked with her on several investigations. Lovely woman and very good at her job. Is there an issue?'

'She has a stalker. A man who is watching her and sending her gifts, and who I believe is capable of much worse. In fact, it's possible he might already have killed.'

DCI Barker's face registered her shock. It was subtle. Three decades in the police force made your reactions pretty muted to most things, but Harrison had surprised her.

'This man, he needs to be handled carefully,' Harrison said to her.

'You have a name?' DCI Barker asked.

'Tanya knows him. He was the boyfriend in a murder case she worked last year.'

'Was he a suspect?'

'I'm not sure. She doesn't think the case has been solved.'

'So why haven't you gone to the SIO?'

"I have to leave town. I need someone to keep an eye on her and find out as much as they can about this man. She's going to stay with a friend for a bit, but he knows where she works. He'll find her again.'

'OK. I'll speak to Tanya, make sure she's safe, and get the SIO's name. You said the first thing you wanted to ask me?'

'Yes, as I said, I need to go out of town, to Cambridgeshire. I helped on a case at the weekend, and they want me to assist with the interviews.'

'You don't need my permission for that.'

'No, but I want to take Jack with me. The DCI there needs an extra pair of experienced hands.'

'Do you know how busy we are here?' DCI Barker shook her head. 'I can't go loaning my good officers out to other constabularies just because they're short staffed.'

'There's an ulterior motive as well, it's also to help Jack out,' Harrison continued. He wasn't in the least surprised by her reaction, and he didn't blame her. 'You know how much he's struggled with Marie's postnatal depression. She won't ask for help or allow anyone to come and stay to give her a break, but her parents live just outside of Cambridge. This is the ideal opportunity for him to persuade her to go and visit her parents while he's working up there for the week. They haven't been able to see Daniel yet, it's a win-win, and you said he needed a holiday.'

'Does he think that will work?'

'Well, I haven't actually told him yet. I thought I should run it by you first because I didn't want him to get his hopes up.'

'Harrison Lane, you certainly know how to do emotional blackmail.' DCI Barker thrummed her fingers on her desk. 'OK, in principle. He's working on stuff that can be carried by DC Oaks in his absence. But it would only be a week.'

Harrison gave her one of his best smiles.

'Thank you, and I promise it will be just one week. Will you keep an eye on Tanya?'

'Yes, I will. I'm not having her life ruined by some pervert.' DCI Barker scribbled something on the notepad by her side. Then she looked up with a cheeky smile on her face and a raised eyebrow. 'You're very concerned about Dr Jones all of a sudden. Getting better acquainted, are we? About time.'

'I'm just helping her out. She's scared.' Harrison stood to leave.

DCI Barker's smile grew wider.

'Mmm, that sounds like a guilty man's excuse.'

'I wouldn't take advantage of this situation.' Harrison looked at her seriously.

'I know you wouldn't, Harrison, but maybe she'd be quite open to you getting to know her a bit better. It's about time you put the single women in this station out of their misery.'

It was Harrison's turn to look surprised. Sandra Barker watched as he struggled to come back with a reply before giving up.

'Thank you for your help,' he mumbled instead, and pulled the office door open to escape.

The DCI sighed with satisfaction at his exit. She lived in hope that he'd chill out at last. Tanya was a strong woman. If anyone could win him over, then it would be her.

Harrison needed to get back on firmer ground and so he pushed the conversation he'd just had with the DCI out of his head and went straight to Jack Salter's desk.

'All right, doc?' Jack beamed as he arrived.

Jack was a little sceptical when Harrison told him the plan, but he called Marie straight away while he was still with him. He repeated the words that Harrison had suggested he use, making it sound as though it had been her suggestion and that she'd be doing her parents the favour by taking their grandson to see them. The smile that lit up Jack's face, and the thumbs up he gave to Harrison, told him that Marie had agreed. They would all leave tonight, ready for Jack and Harrison to start work in the morning.

. . .

After work, Harrison picked up Tanya and took her back to his flat to collect her things. She was quieter than usual, subdued.

'Thanks for getting DCI Barker involved,' she said to him. 'She's already spoken to the SIO on the case, and I was right, nobody's been charged.'

'Did he say anything about your stalker?'

Tanya had been quiet, but when she spoke, her voice dropped further in volume.

'Yeah. He said his gut told him that the boyfriend killed her, but they had no evidence and he'd got an alibi. The SIO reckons that the man who gave him his alibi is lying, but their hands are tied. He hasn't given up on it though and is very interested in what's happening with me. He's going to do a renewed push, check out past relationships, re-interview him.'

'I'm sorry I have to leave London for a few days, but DCI Barker has promised to be there and help you, so if anything happens you must promise to call her.'

'Yeah, she's given me her mobile. I'll be fine. He's been hanging around for weeks now, it's not like he's going to suddenly do something.'

Tanya didn't sound so convinced about the last statement, and Harrison wasn't either. He reached out and took her hand.

'Please, Tanya, promise me you'll also call me

if you're scared—after you've called 999 of course. That if anything happens you won't ignore it, you'll report it. I'm not that far away. If you need me, I can come back.'

She'd looked at her hand in his, and then up to his face, her blue eyes full of tears. 'Thank you,' she said, and then she'd brushed the tears away and stood up straight. 'Don't you worry. He's not going to scare me. I will not be his next victim. He's picked on the wrong girl.'

17

DCI Whittaker was ecstatic at the news that Harrison and Jack were coming to help with the case. He'd not held out too much hope because he knew how strapped everyone was with staff. When Harrison and Jack arrived at the station in the morning, he had everything prepared to give them a full brief and hit the ground running. All he needed to do was handle a disgruntled DS Brian O'Neil, who'd taken the announcement of their coming as a personal affront.

Jack was staying with the in-laws. He'd left a smiling Marie sitting watching her parents cooing over their son, while her mother intermittently stopped cuddling him to fuss over her. He hadn't felt this relieved in months. It literally felt like a ton of weight, responsibility, and worry had been lifted from his shoulders. He was as light as a feather.

Jack arrived at the Cambridgeshire Constabulary headquarters in the Hinchingbrooke Business Park. There were fields surrounding the buildings and large, open-air car parks. Trees framed the site on two sides of its triangular area. A huge sky of blue with an accent of white hung above the landscape. It had been a while since Jack had visited this area of Britain, he'd forgotten just how big and open it was, compared to the squashed skyline of London.

Jack had just turned off his engine when he saw Harrison swing his Harley into the car park. The relief he felt now, which was down to Harrison's idea to get Marie up here, meant he could have walked straight up to him and given him a hug—but of course he didn't. He did allow himself a secret laugh at the image in his head of Harrison's reaction if he had.

Jack had already read the post-mortem, Harrison's offender profile, and the reports from the SIOs. It was immediately obvious that they didn't have a clue at this stage who the murderer was, but there were plenty of suspects. He also needed to try to get inside Harrison's head to work out what it was he was thinking—not a straightforward task. It was clear he had some theories of his own and wasn't convinced the new SIO was going to take any notice of theirs.

The board that met them in the incident room, plastered with dozens of photographs, names, and question marks, was a testament to the lack of solid leads.

The second they'd walked into the room, DS Brian O'Neil had intercepted them.

'Dr Lane.' He nodded. 'And DS Salter, I presume?' His tone was tense. There was no smile or outstretched hand.

Jack immediately thrust his hand out to greet him. It hung there midair for a few moments, before DS O'Neil realised there were eyes in the room, watching. He took Jack's hand firmly, shook it once, and then dropped it.

'We've been making good progress and have several suspects,' he started.

Harrison wondered if he realised how defensive he sounded. He didn't know DS O'Neil very well but didn't need to spend more than a few minutes with him to know he was someone who didn't do subtlety and social etiquette. It helped explain why he hadn't climbed the ranks sooner.

'The DCI wants me to hold a briefing for

you,' O'Neil continued. There was an unsubtle sneer in his voice. 'I'll get my team together. We need to keep it short because we're all busy. If you go into the briefing room,' he tipped his head towards a doorway at the other end of the room, 'we'll join you.'

Jack looked at Harrison and raised an eyebrow. When they'd reached the privacy of the briefing room, he said what he was thinking.

'Warm welcome! Had hoped there might be a bit more appreciation for the extra support, but I guess we're interfering outsiders from London.'

'I don't think DS O'Neil is particularly warm to anyone,' Harrison replied, remembering the briefing he'd given to the team the last time he was here.

'I guess he's had his nose put out of joint by the DCI asking us to help. Made it look like he wasn't capable of running the investigation. I reckon I'd be a bit annoyed,' Jack added.

'He isn't capable,' Harrison replied in his usual matter-of-fact way. He settled himself into one of the chairs at the far end of the meeting table.

Jack could always rely on him to tell it how it was.

A few minutes later Harrison spotted the DCI

heading their way, closely followed by a constable carrying a tray laden with coffees and water, and following up the rear a grim-faced DS O'Neil and two other detectives.

Once introductions were out of the way, DS O'Neil stood up and began.

'Paul was with his girlfriend, Gabby Peterson, a jockey at the Three Oaks Stables the night before his murder. They both got up early in the morning and went out on exercise with the horses, before Paul went back to his cottage alone. That was the last time she saw him. Paul's phone GPS shows that a few hours later, he left his cottage and went to the barn on the edge of Fordham Woods. The phone and car remained there until we found them.'

'Could I get into the barn as a matter of urgency?' Harrison spoke up.

'Absolutely. We've done a lot of the forensic work there already. You can get in this morning,' DCI Whittaker answered. DS O'Neil ground his teeth and continued.

'Some of Paul's friends said he had a very public row with an Alex Michaels, another jockey, at the last big meet. He accused Alex of riding dangerously and the two were nearly sanctioned for fighting, but friends intervened, and the officials let it go. Gabby suggested Alex is a bit of a wild card and known for not only being tough on his mounts but also for cutting up some of the other horses on the track. We've requested he talk to us. He's at a race today, but we should get him tomorrow.'

'And the other suspects?' Jack asked innocently.

The DCI looked at DS O'Neil and raised an eyebrow. The detective gave Jack a dirty look. He wondered if he'd said something wrong, so qualified himself.

'You said you have several suspects.'

'We have potential suspects,' DS O'Neil finally replied. 'Craig Matlock is holding back. We think he must be one of The Horsemen as it's his barn, but he won't give us the names of any of the others and claims to have no idea why Paul was killed. My money is this whole thing is related to that secret society of theirs.' He threw a glance at Harrison. 'Dr Lane said they use scented oils to attract horses, or repel them. What if someone wanted to get hold of those oils so they could use them? There's big money in horse racing. If you wanted to stop a horse from leaving the stalls, why not use the oil? It would be pretty much undetectable and have an impact on who wins. Or maybe Paul had already been trying that trick himself and either got found out or got cold feet. We could be looking at organised crime gang involvement. There was that tip off last year that one of the OCGs out of Manchester was involved in race fixing.' O'Neil looked triumphantly at Harrison, his boss and Jack.

'Good work Brian, it's certainly plausible. We need to look at who was set to gain or lose from that, and if there's any links between Paul and known OCG members,' DCI Whittaker said.

Harrison said nothing.

He'd been skim reading Gabby Phillip's interview transcript. It wasn't so much what she'd said as what she hadn't said. After they'd been to the barn, their first visit needed to be with her. He waited for the meeting to break-up and it was just him, Jack, and the DCI left in the room.

'Do we have permission to interview who we want?' he asked.

'Yes, absolutely, as long as it's all logged officially, and you tell Brian. I know he's a bit prickly about you being here, you've got to understand that I had given this to him and it's his territory, but if things get too difficult, come straight to me. I'll make sure you both have all the clearances, and all the team, and forensics know.'

'So, who have you got your eyes on as our first interview?' Jack turned to Harrison once the DCI had left. 'You don't ask a question unless there's a reason behind it.'

'Gabby Peterson, Paul's girlfriend. She was upset when they first interviewed her, and I think they went easy on the questioning. But first we need to get to the barn.'

18

Jack drove them to the barn at Fordham Woods, aided by Harrison's directions and his satnav.

'So tell me about The Horsemen,' he said to Harrison in the car on the way, 'What's it all about?'

'It was an ancient society, not just from round here, but other parts of the UK, including Scotland. It was all about sharing the trade secrets of being a horseman and ploughman, when they were essential to farming and society. They formed a brotherhood to help each other, swore oaths and carried out rituals. A bit like a superstitious trades union, although they also shared practical cures when modern medicine hadn't yet come about. It's thought the origins go back centuries. If you had all the secrets then you could probably make a better income than those who weren't in the brotherhood. They had recipes for scented oils which could be used to control horses. Powerful stuff, if those became common knowledge they could be used wrongly, and so they had to swear an oath not to tell the secrets. The penalty was death.'

'So it could be that Paul was killed by the group because he talked?'

'It's a possibility but I don't think so.'

'O'Neil's theory sounds good. If those scented oils could be used in a way to impact a race, then it could be a motive.'

Harrison was silent for a few moments.

'It doesn't fit with what they did to him, cutting out his heart. I still think it's related to fear and not greed.'

'And the toad bone?'

'You could be a Toad man without being a Horseman, but the two were often linked. Superstition said that the bone was what gave the powers. Many thought it was linked to the devil.'

'Can't see the attraction of having a bit of dead toad around my neck, personally,' said Jack.

'No, but think how many people carried around dead rabbit's feet to bring them luck.'

'Well if Paul Lester's experience is anything to

go by, perhaps that's why toad bones never caught on as good luck charms – didn't bring him much luck did it?'

When they arrived at the barn, there was one lone forensics van there, and just two staff on site. Jack knew how Harrison liked to work and so he suggested he spoke to the forensics team while Harrison went in. It would give him a head start and the quiet he needed to focus.

Inside, the barn was bleached out with bright lights the team had rigged up so they could see into every nook and cranny of the structure. Harrison turned off all the extra lighting so that the barn was reduced to a soft glow inside. It was important to understand the conditions on the day Paul was killed. What could be seen, what couldn't. He'd turn the lights back on later when looking for details.

Harrison preferred to get into a crime scene as soon as possible after the event. It wasn't just the visuals, but the smell and feel of the place as well. All of these were triggers to mood and atmosphere which could affect a person's behaviours and reactions. Every stimulus could give a clue as to what had gone on. The barn had been full of forensics staff for the past two days, so its original ambience would have been disturbed. However, he could still get a good feel for the place.

Harrison closed the door to the barn. Jack and the two forensics officers were far enough away that their voices were a murmur that could be filtered out. He closed his eyes, cleared his head, and brought his focus into connection with the here and now. He wanted the barn to seep into him so he could feel its energy and witness what it had seen that day.

The first thing that struck Harrison was the area to which his eyes were drawn once he'd re-opened them. It had the feel of being in a church with an altar. The barn lights were directed so as to pull your view to the far end where a large wooden table was set up with big candlesticks on either side. Above the table were hung two horse skulls. In front was a seating area with large wooden backed pews running along the left wall. They looked like they'd probably been bought after the closure of a local church. On the other side was a pile of straw bales, possibly used as further seating. Maybe there was a hierarchy in the society, the leaders sitting on the benches and the new recruits atop the straw bales.

To the right of this area, behind the bales, was a giant pile of hay and straw as though somebody had scattered it ready for a large gathering of horses. It must have been over four feet thick. This pile was only visible if you walked to the right, around the stacked bales, and couldn't be seen at all from the 'altar' area.

Closer to this pile, a dark, almost black sticky pool showed where Paul had his heart cut from him. In between that and the hay, was a series of markers left by the forensics team. Harrison knew what had been here, he'd seen the photographs. A long length of rope had lain, stretched and curled like a basking snake, only this snake had a noose instead of a head. It was now back at the lab, being combed for DNA.

Harrison hadn't moved far from the doorway, but he could see almost everything in the barn. It wasn't a particularly large area, and while the shadows were soft around the walls, it would be hard for anyone to hide in here, unless they'd climbed into the hayloft. He would try up there in a few moments.

The air was mostly what you'd expect, a dusty hay smell wrapped in musty damp wood, but the iron laden odour of dried blood gave it an edge.

When he reached the hay, there was a pile of forensic labelled bags, around the size of bin bags, on the floor. Several were already filled. The SOCOs had quite literally drawn the short straw and were having to bag all the hay so they could ensure nothing was hidden within it, and in case it would be needed later. Question was, why was it there in the first place? Harrison had a strong suspicion. He looked up. A large beam stretched across the roof of the barn. He needed to get up into the hayloft.

Harrison climbed the ladder, which was positioned to the right and led straight up to an area that covered roughly a third of the barn's size at the far end. It was empty. The only thing he could find was a thin piece of rope tied to one of the vertical beams at the edge of the hayloft, and above that, a large metal ring. When he stood on the edge next to them, he was looking down directly onto the pile of hay below. Up above ran the large timber beam. There was no doubt in Harrison's mind that this was where Paul had been hung from. The thin piece of rope would have held the noose secure, ready to be used, and the ring would have been where the other end of the rope was tied, with the beam the hanging point. This wasn't a quick opportune murder. The hanging noose was a fixture. The ring had been there some time, he could tell that from its colouring and that of the wood where it had been screwed in. Harrison knew exactly why it was there. Question was, why had Paul died here?

He heard the metal mechanism on the barn door handle squeak, and it creaked open to show Jack and the two forensics officers walking in, deep in conversation. Jack looked around the barn.

'Harrison?'

'Here,' he replied, pulling the gaze of all three men upwards. 'Was there any evidence that things had been removed before you got here?' he asked the SOCOs as he climbed back down the ladder.

'Not that we're aware,' one of them replied, 'but we weren't first response, just got called in today.'

This confirmed Harrison's suspicions that they really had drawn the short straw, probably new recruits. He'd have to speak to the crime scene manager.

By the time he'd reached the ground floor, the bright lights had been switched back on. He spent a few minutes looking around, but after all the activity that had been in the barn in the last forty-eight hours, he didn't expect to find much in the way of signs. Instead, while Jack was being given a guided tour, he slipped outside.

Harrison started a slow clockwise walk around the barn. Clockwise because that took him first to the most sheltered side, away from where the cars were parked. Again, he didn't hope for too much in the way of tracks to see, there would have been too many officers walking around the site, but he was looking for something else.

Harrison almost missed it. The hole had been plugged by a small piece of wood which nearly matched the barn wall. Having the bright lights on inside helped him, because a tiny amount of light seeped out where the wooden plug didn't quite fill the hole. He stopped immediately and studied the ground. The rain would have obliterated any tracks from the night Paul died, but there could be signs that someone came to this spot regularly. The mud was indeed compacted, and the grass trodden into it. The area definitely looked more worn. Harrison wanted to pull the piece of wood out and peer in to see what view it gave, but it could potentially hold DNA evidence of the man who'd put it there. Instead, he carried on walking, searching for anywhere else that someone could see into the barn.

By the time he'd circled back to the door, it was obvious that was the only spot. He went back inside.

'I need one of you to bag something. Could have DNA of the killer on it,' he announced to the forensics officers who were still stood talking to Jack and looked up at him surprised.

'OK, I'll get a smaller bag, or is it a big

object?' one of the young men replied. He looked fresh out of school with keen, bright eyes. Harrison suspected they'd not yet broken him in on anything too gruesome yet. He still had the enthusiasm of someone who thought he could make a difference, not the resigned professionalism of those who had seen it all before.

'What have you found?' Jack asked.

'I'll show you,' Harrison replied, walking back outside.

All four trooped around the back of the barn. Harrison was careful to lead them a couple of feet away from the wall, so that when they got there, they didn't tread on the ground around the hole.

'The mud has been compacted. Someone stood here more than once. There's a hole, which they plug with wood so it doesn't get discovered. I need you to bag it so we can see what it is they look at.'

Jack took a few photographs on his phone, and one of the SOCOs stepped forward and tweezer'd the wood out of the hole and into a bag. He stepped aside so that Harrison could take a look. The hole gave the perfect view of the 'altar' area in the barn. Whoever stood there would have been able to watch all the ceremonies and meetings and could even just about see up to where the hangman's noose had been attached to the wooden pillar.

'Most of the ceremonies would have been at night, he'd have watched in the dark so they wouldn't see the hole being opened up,' Harrison said as he stepped away to let Jack look through. 'This man was clearly obsessed with The Horsemen.'

'How would he have known when they were holding their meetings?' Jack asked. 'I assume that nothing else went on in this barn, no naked yoga or anything like that?'

The two forensics officers smirked, but quickly wiped the smiles from their faces when they saw Harrison wasn't laughing.

'No,' he said in the same serious tone, completely ignoring the joke. 'Nothing else could have gone on here. It would have compromised their secrecy, so that's a good question. How did he know when only the members received invites? Answer that and we find the killer.'

19

Jack and Harrison left the two young forensics officers to carry on with their hay bagging, while they went to interview Gabby Peterson, Paul's girlfriend. She didn't live at Three Oaks Stables, but with her parents in a small village about ten miles away. The roads were starting to look more familiar to Harrison, and while Jack drove, he mulled over his question of how the killer could have known when meetings were being held.

'You could at least let me get a word in. You never stop the banter, do you?' Jack broke the silence in the car.

Harrison turned to look at him. There was a broad grin on his face.

'Marie enjoying being at her parents?'

Harrison asked, suddenly mindful that he hadn't enquired how she was getting on.

'Absolutely, can't thank you enough for the suggestion. It gave her the excuse to come see them and they're loving having her there with Daniel.'

'It will help her feel like he's really part of the family, to see them with him and to be in their lives.'

'Yeah, I can see that. Her mother won't put him down, so it's giving her the break she needed. They've even dug out some old toys Marie had as a baby. It's given me a break too. I've not had to worry about them all morning.'

There was a brief lull again, this time while Jack thought about something. His words had triggered Harrison's thoughts to turn to Tanya. When he'd woken up this morning, he'd texted her to check everything was alright, but there was a constant worry at the back of his mind. He felt London pulling him back, like a child tugging on his sleeve.

'Is it hard having to investigate murders like this, you know, when it's a hanging?' Jack broke the silence again and Harrison felt him throw a glance away from the road and in his direction.

'Because of my mum, you mean? No. I never think like that,' he replied.

'Did you ever know your dad?' Jack asked.

'No. I have no idea who he is, or even where my mother met him.'

'Not even any suspicions?' Jack pressed, amazed. 'Your mum was blonde right, and you're clearly not.'

'That much is evident, but it still doesn't help with finding who my father might be, other than the fact he almost certainly wasn't pale blond, short and puny.'

That made Jack laugh.

'He may not even know I exist. He was never in my life.'

'I'm sorry, it must be hard. Look, I've been thinking, I really want to help you find your mum's killer. If you believe there's been a crime, then we're duty bound to investigate it.'

'It's been over fifteen years.'

'It doesn't matter how long, you know that.'

'They said it was suicide, the local police weren't interested.'

'Yeah, well, I looked at the reports. There were inconsistencies, flags that would have told me it wasn't.'

Harrison looked at Jack now. He was focused on driving, his face serious as he turned the car into a residential road. The satnav announced that they'd reached their destination and Jack pulled over, switched the engine off, and twisted round so he could face Harrison.

'I hope you don't mind that I looked, but once you'd told me, I thought I should see if you had a case.'

'I know she was murdered,' Harrison replied.

'I believe you, Harrison. There were defence marks on her arms for one thing.'

For the first time, Jack saw the impenetrable cool of Dr Harrison Lane waver. He said nothing, but Jack suspected that was because he was struggling to speak. It might be over fifteen years, but the grief was still there to see. Harrison turned his head away.

'Look, I'm serious. I want to help you, and get justice for your mother. When we get back to London, I'll pull in some favours and see what we can find.'

'Thanks, Jack,' Harrison finally said. 'I appreciate you believing me.'

'First time we worked together, I was told you're always right and to trust you,' Jack replied in his more usual tone, and he smiled as he got out of the car.

They were in a small road of semi-detached houses, built in the 1950s when gardens were big enough to fit more than just a couple of plant pots and a chair in them. The Peterson's house was number 12, a small metal gate lead into a lawned front garden with flower beds cut into it and a rosebush in the middle on each side. It was a classic British residential street. Sparrows were sat in a row on the guttering, arguing and squabbling, while below them a blackbird flung leaf debris around in the flower bed, searching for worms and grubs. There was a porch attached to the front of the house, which wasn't locked. As they walked towards it, the blackbird flew up, squawking a warning, and Jack stepped inside to ring the front doorbell.

Inside the porch, Harrison could see riding boots lined up with walking shoes and wellies. His mind went back to Paul Lester's hallway.

The door was opened by a man in his fifties with a full head of greying hair and a friendly face that was just the wrong side of handsome. He was in jeans and a green Ralph Lauren woollen jumper with a checked shirt underneath.

'Mr Peterson?' Jack asked. 'I'm DS Jack Salter, and this is Dr Harrison Lane. We're hoping to speak with Gabby about Paul Lester.'

'She's already given a statement, you know,' her father answered, not aggressively, but he was clearly concerned about the whole situation and what impact it might have on his daughter.

'It's OK, Dad,' a voice came from behind

him, and Gabby appeared at the door alongside him. 'I'll talk to them. If it helps catch Paul's killer, then I'll answer as many questions as they need.'

Frederick Peterson stepped aside and waved them both in.

'I'll put the kettle on,' he said, and disappeared into the kitchen ahead of them, while Jack and Harrison followed Gabby into their sitting-room on the right-hand side. Gabby was a petite redhead in her early twenties, with a pixie face. Despite her slight build, Harrison suspected she was strong. Her active work with horses would ensure good fitness levels, and she looked like the kind of girl who took care of herself and didn't abuse her body. Today she had dark circles under her eyes, accentuated by her pale skin, from where she'd been crying.

'I can't believe that anyone would do this to Paul,' she said, as they each chose somewhere to sit. The words hung in the air between them, as they did at so many meetings like this after a murder.

'We've read your statement,' Jack began, settling into the large leather sofa and pulling out his notebook. 'We've got just a few more questions, if that's OK?'

Gabby nodded and immediately began playing with the sleeve of her jumper. Harrison looked around the sitting-room. It was stylish, in a traditional sense, with a nice, polished mahogany sideboard. Along the mantlepiece was a row of wooden ornaments, Harrison guessed Mr Peterson must be into wood turning. There was a selection of family photographs—it appeared Gabby had an older brother—and a pile of *Woman & Home* magazines on the coffee table along with an iPad.

It didn't look as though the Petersons were particularly horsey people until Gabby came along. There were photographs of her as a young girl atop a pony with rosettes and a more recent one of her on-board a racehorse at one of the big meetings. Harrison wasn't sure which course.

'We understand Paul had a row with Alex Michaels. How was he after that?'

'He was fine. He just thought Alex was a dick. Sorry.' She looked embarrassed for her language. 'I mean, he didn't have much time for him, you know? Thought he was an idiot.'

'Why was that?' Jack pressed.

'Alex is really ambitious. He doesn't give a toss about anyone but himself and winning races. That goes for the horses too. Paul hated that he used to whip them too much. He got disciplined and suspended a couple of times over it. Paul always said that jockeys should rely on balance and rhythm to get them over the finish line, and that using the whip was the sign of a bad rider who wasn't in tune with his horse.'

'Is that why they argued?'

'Not the last time, no. Paul said Alex had drifted off his line purposely to block him. The stewards called it careless riding, but Paul accused him of being dangerous and trying to stop him from getting through. Another horse won. Alex wasn't ever going to lead the field, but he wanted to make sure Paul didn't.'

'So there was a personal rivalry?'

'Definitely. They both trained at the same time, but Alex drinks too much and was banned a couple of years ago for a few months after they found cocaine in a pre-race drugs test. Paul was a better jockey and Alex always struggled to keep his weight down.'

Gabby's father popped his head around the door at this point.

'Tea or coffee, gents?'

'A coffee would be lovely, thank you,' Jack replied.

'I don't suppose you have any herbal teas, do you?' Harrison queried.

'Yes, we've got mint or chamomile in the cupboard,' Gabby replied, as much to her nonplussed father as Harrison. 'Mum likes it.'

'Then I'll have a mint, thank you,' Harrison said.

'Just normal tea for me, please, Dad,' Gabby added.

Harrison turned to Gabby when her dad had gone.

'Were you aware of the group that Paul belonged to? The Horsemen?' He watched Gabby's face closely. Her face had hardened ever so slightly. There was tension in her jaw and she twisted her sleeve hard.

'Yes,' she said.

'Do you know if Alex was in that group?' Jack asked.

'No. Definitely not. Paul wouldn't talk about it much. I knew it existed, but it was all top secret. The one thing I do know is that they were all Paul's friends who belonged to it, jockeys and those who worked in racing, and who he considered were good blokes and good to horses. Paul loved his horses.' Gabby looked upset again, and they gave her a moment.

'How was Paul in the days before his death? Was he any different to usual?' Jack asked.

'He was fine.' She shrugged. 'We were both riding at a meet this weekend and he'd suggested we stayed over in a hotel together. We were planning ahead, talking about summer holidays.'

‘Is there anything that seemed to be worrying him? Anyone else that he’d had a run in with?’

At this point, Mr Peterson returned with a clinking tray of drinks.

‘I brought sugar, as I wasn’t sure if you took it,’ he said, handing a mug to each of them. ‘Paul was a good lad, you know,’ he added. ‘Didn’t deserve this.’ He shook his head and looked sadly at his daughter.

‘Yes, he wasn’t aggressive, didn’t go round picking fights or anything,’ Gabby said now, animated. ‘He was a gentle guy… it’s just he couldn’t stand horse cruelty.’

‘We’re not suggesting he wasn’t, Gabby, but someone wanted to kill him and so we need to know about every disagreement he had in order to try to find that man.’

Gabby looked down at her hands.

‘We have to ask you this, but I need to confirm your whereabouts on Friday evening,’ Jack asked.

‘I was here. Went to bed early, didn’t I dad?’

‘Yes. She did,’ Mr Peterson confirmed. ‘They get them working very early, you know. And it’s often long days, it’s no wonder she’s tired out. Some days we don’t see her at all because she’s up and gone before we’re even awake. That evening she was in bed early, exhausted.’

'Good that you're in a nice quiet street here then, so you don't get woken up.' Jack said.

Gabby's father smiled.

'Yes it's quieter out back, but Gabby likes her old room at the front don't you love. Once you're asleep that's you gone until the alarm isn't it?'

Gabby smiled at her father and he slipped out the room.

'They worry about me,' she said to Jack and Harrison. 'Actually, there was one other thing I forgot to mention to the other officers, but I'm not sure if it went anywhere. It was with a trainer and Paul told me not to tell anyone.' She looked up at the two men's faces. 'He found out that one of the trainers was using EPO with his horses, to boost their red blood cell counts. I can't remember its full name. People use a version called Epogen, you'd get given it if you were anaemic. Lance Armstrong the cyclist was supposed to have used it because the more red blood cells you have, the more oxygen there is. It's a performance enhancer, and it's difficult to test for because basically it's just encouraging a natural process. Paul saw blood coming from a horse's nostrils after a race and the jockey let slip. It's dangerous for the horse because it can encourage them to push their bodies too hard, and sometimes it thickens their blood making heart attacks more likely. Paul told the trainer he wouldn't ride for him anymore, and threatened to report him unless he stopped, but I'm not sure what happened.'

'Which trainer was this?'

'Gavin Simons at Belle View Stables.'

Jack scribbled down the name.

'Actually, I heard he's just been banned for ketamine.'

'Ketamine?' Jack queried.

'They found ketamine in one of his horses's bloods prior to a race meet about a week ago. No one was massively surprised. He's not got the greatest reputation round here. It's a sedative and used by vets to tranquillise horses. There's gossip about race fixing, but I've no idea if that's true.'

'I've come across ketamine, or Special K, Donkey Dust or Kit Kat, whatever it's being called, among club goers. I've seen people KO'd by it and ending up with a catheter for life because it wrecked their bladder,' Jack said. 'It's strong stuff, but you quickly develop a tolerance and users end up needing more and more. Is it used locally as a recreational drug?'

Gabby shrugged.

'I know some people take it, it's cheaper than some of the other stuff, but just to be clear, Paul never did drugs.'

Jack nodded now.

'Did you know Paul received an invitation to go to a meeting of The Horsemen the day he was killed?' asked Harrison.

There it went again, the tightening of her jaw.

'No. He didn't say anything.' Gabby replied curtly.

'Did you ever know when he was getting the invites? Did he show them to you?'

'No.'

'Did you not want to join?' Harrison asked.

Gabby looked him in the face.

'It was men only. Some crap about it being traditional. But there are lots of things that were traditional, doesn't mean it's right.'

'So you wanted to join?' Harrison pressed.

Gabby shrugged and looked away, taking a deep breath and sitting up rigidly. Harrison didn't miss the body language.

'Do you know who's in the group?' Jack asked now.

'Not for sure, no. Like I said, Paul wouldn't talk about it with me. I think membership was supposed to be secret.'

'Could you hazard a guess as to who might be involved?' Jack pushed.

'Well, an obvious one would be Craig, Craig Matlock, they're always in each other's pockets. He's the first number Paul dials when he wants to go out for a drink.' Gabby thought for a few moments. 'Plus, possibly Luke Spencer and Harvey Ball. He hung out with them a lot at race meets, but I don't even know how many were in the group.'

'That's helpful. They might know something so it's important we speak to them,' said Jack.

'This might sound like a strange question, but bear with me. Did Paul know anyone who was particularly superstitious or a bit OCD about things?' Harrison asked.

'There're quite a few OCD jockeys. You have to be to make sure you stay the right weight, plus most of us have our good luck charms or routines. Can't think of anyone who is overly superstitious though.'

'Do you?' Harrison asked.

'Do I what?'

'Have your good luck charms and routines?'

Gabby's eyes flickered over his face, looking for the motivation behind his question.

'Nothing major,' she replied, 'just the usual stuff.'

'Sorry, what is the usual stuff?' Jack asked now.

'You know, not letting my hat or reins touch the ground before a race and carrying a lucky charm. Some people have to get dressed in a certain order. I don't like to see a single magpie on the way, my mum taught me that. One for sorrow.'

'That's quite a few superstitions,' Harrison said.

Gabby shrugged again and looked at him as if to say *so what*?

'Is there anybody else who Paul might have had an issue with?' Jack asked.

'He was popular, people liked him. They admired him. He was so good with horses. Someone might have been jealous of that, but there's no one in particular. Sorry, no.'

'That's OK, you've been very helpful.' Jack smiled reassuringly at her and threw a glance at Harrison to see if he had any more questions.

'Thank you for your time and sorry for your loss,' Harrison said, and rose from the chair to leave. Jack quickly drunk his coffee.

'Actually, now I think about it,' Gabby suddenly said. 'Gavin Simons is quite superstitious, he's Irish and I remember seeing him with shamrocks and horseshoes on his hat at one of the race meets. Also, I heard he has some weird ritual he does before each race, but I can't remember what it is.'

'Thank you,' Jack replied. 'That's very useful to know.'

As Jack and Harrison walked down the front path, Jack turned round and looked at the house. Harrison raised his eyebrows quizzically at him.

'I'm thinking it's not too difficult to climb out your bedroom window onto that porch and disappear off without your parents realising you're not still in bed sleeping.' Jack said to Harrison.

'Agreed. She also wasn't a fan of The Horsemen, that was clear from her body language.'

'I don't think we can ignore Gabby Peterson as a potential suspect. Our list is getting longer,' Jack said with a sigh.

20

It wasn't a difficult decision as to where to go next. Gavin Simons hadn't been on the suspects board back at the incident room, but after what Gabby had told them, Harrison and Jack were very interested in talking to him.

Jack phoned in to speak to DS O'Neil, who didn't seem all that interested in what he had to say.

'We've had to release Craig Matlock, he's still refusing to tell us who the other Horsemen are. We've also found out that Richard Carter, the owner of Three Oaks Stables, has prior for assault. We're pushing him up the list,' the DS told Jack. He was on speakerphone and Harrison rolled his eyes at the tone of his voice.

'Anything to get one over on DS James I

think,' said Harrison, once they'd finished the call. 'The man has a massive inferiority complex which is probably why he drinks.'

'I drink because I like it,' smirked Jack. 'Why have you never had a drink? Your life so black and white and stress-less that you don't need to let your hair down?'

'I haven't said I've never had a drink,' Harrison said seriously. 'I went through a phase of using alcohol as an emotional crutch. It didn't get me anywhere, just made things worse. I don't miss it, and I don't like losing control.'

'Really? I would never have said that,' Jack replied in a friendly but sarcastic mutter.

Harrison chose to ignore him.

When they arrived at Belle View Stables, the contrast with Three Oaks was immediately obvious to Harrison. Even the sign carrying the stable name was tacky, carrying the message that everyone can be a racehorse owner. All you had to do was join the Belle View Club. The stable block was tired and there was no pool or solarium here. It comprised four rows of stables, with a large building that housed the tack room, staff room, and feed store. It was more like the standard stables that Harrison had been to before, more chilled, but undoubtedly less money flowed through its yard. The staff seemed younger too, no matching livery for the grooms. They wore jeans or jodhpurs. A sign for 'Office' pointed towards the house, and that's where the two men headed.

Jack knocked, and they entered into an untidy melee of office and horse racing. The walls were full of photographs, mostly of the man who sat behind the big desk in front of them, standing next to various racehorses. Piles of paperwork, books, and an assortment of riding equipment were stacked around the edges of the room. Plus, there was a large neon green leprechaun and a top hat smothered in Irish shamrocks, and fake horseshoes. Almost certainly the hat which Gabby had mentioned. The large wooden desk itself was relatively tidy and as they approached, the man behind it jumped up with an extended hand of welcome.

'Mr Simons?' Jack asked.

'Yes, Mr Wilson?' he replied, and then didn't wait for the answer. 'You're a little early. I was going to have one of my team meet you, but welcome.' He was a well-built man with a large bulldog head, thick neck, and close-cropped hair. He looked more like a rugby prop forward than the jockey he'd once been.

'Ah no, sorry, I'm DS Jack Salter and this is Dr Harrison Lane. We're investigating the murder of Paul Lester.'

Gavin Simons's hand shot back as though he'd been burned. The change in his face was unmistakable, and although he tried to regain his composure, both Harrison and Jack noticed the sudden panic.

'I see, well I've got an appointment in,' he checked his watch, 'fifteen minutes. It's a very important business meeting and I can't miss it.'

'That's all right, Mr Simons, we won't keep you. We just have a few questions to ask.'

Gavin Simons was clearly running through the scenarios in his mind. What he should say, what he shouldn't say, what if he refused to say anything. In the end he plonked back down in his chair wearily and motioned for Jack and Harrison to take a seat.

'I'm not sure if you were aware that Mr Lester was found murdered on Wicken Fen on Saturday morning?' Jack started.

'Yes, I heard,' said Gavin. And then added as an afterthought, 'Tragic.'

'We understand that you and the victim had a falling out?'

'No, well… yes we did, but I didn't kill him if that's what you're saying.'

'I'm not saying that you did, Mr Simons, I'm just asking you about the nature of your relationship with Mr Lester.'

'He's ridden for me in the past. We mix in the same circles at meets. It's a small community.'

'Why did you argue?'

'We didn't argue. We had a disagreement. He accused me of something and then, then he threatened me.'

'Threatened you? What physically?'

'No. Threatened to get me into trouble with race authorities. I think he framed me with the ketamine. I didn't give that horse ketamine, I swear it. I'm appealing the ruling.'

'Sorry, could you clarify please, Mr Simons?' Jack played dumb, knowing full well what Gavin was referring to, but wanting his explanation.

'Last week, there was a routine drugs test on one of my horses at a meet and they found ketamine. That horse wasn't given it at my stables, I'm telling you. Do you know how hard I've worked to build this business? I'm in debt up to my eyeballs, mortgaged to the hilt. You get banned for a few months by race authorities on drug charges and it can ruin your business. Horse owners won't trust me. I'm appealing it, but shit sticks.'

'Did you confront Mr Lester about this?'

'We spoke on the phone.'

Harrison hadn't said a word. He was watching the man in front of him closely. His body language, the words he used, the sheen of sweat that was appearing on his forehead. The darting eyes and exaggerated hand movements. This was a man caught in a trap somewhere he knew he shouldn't have been. Jack didn't let up.

'Where were you on Friday evening, Mr Simons?'

'I was here. You ask my staff, they'll have seen me.'

'Are you married?'

'No. Divorced. I live alone in the house.'

'Did you stay at the stables all evening?'

'Yes.'

'And do you have any idea who might want to hurt Paul?'

'No. I didn't see him that often, we weren't close friends. You're better off asking these questions over at Three Oaks Stables. Look, I need to prepare for my meeting now. If there's anything else, then we can talk about it another time.' He stood up to act as a signal he meant it. There was a sliver of desperation in his voice.

'Thank you, Mr Simons. We may well be back as our investigation progresses.'

'No problem,' Gavin replied, but with little

conviction, and smiled as though they had given him a temporary reprieve from the hangman's noose.

'Do you know about The Horsemen? The secret association Paul was part of?' Harrison spoke now for the first time and Gavin Simons turned to look at him.

'Secret association? It's just a bunch of lads meeting up over a few beers to talk horses, isn't it?' He sneered as he said it, and laughed, but the laugh sounded nervous.

'So you are aware of it, then? Do you know who the members are and where they meet?'

Gavin shrugged. 'Not sure, but I think Craig Matlock's involved.'

'How do you know that?' Harrison pushed.

Gavin hesitated, you could almost see his mind working overtime and wishing he'd not even mentioned the name.

'They're friends. Everyone knows that,' he came up with.

Harrison watched his face. His pupils had dilated a little, and his voice was raised very slightly in pitch.

'You're not involved?' He pushed.

A frown jumped onto Gavin's forehead, and he knitted his eyebrows at Harrison.

'No, I don't go in for all that ridiculous so-called secret society stuff.' Gavin waved his hand as if dismissing it.

'But you believe in good luck from leprechauns and shamrocks?' Harrison continued.

'Oh this? I play up to it. You know the luck of the Irish and all that. It's part of the persona.'

There was a knock at the door, and one of the stable lads poked his head around. He was a thin, pale-faced youth with the Caesar cut hairstyle that seemed to be popular among young men again. Harrison couldn't see its appeal, but then he wasn't in his early twenties anymore. He'd stick with his standard crew cut any day. The small horizontal fringe with close shaved sides, reminiscent of the Roman leader, made the lad look like an old-fashioned street stray, rather than the powerful leader it had been inspired by.

'Mr Wilson is here, Gav,' the lad said, eyeballing Harrison and Jack suspiciously.

'Cheers Lewis, I'm coming. Gentlemen, if you wouldn't mind?' He ushered them both out of the door politely, but firmly, following them out and locking it behind him.

'Did you see the shamrocks and leprechaun?' Jack said quietly to Harrison as they left.

'That's just showman superstition, I wouldn't take it seriously,' Harrison replied.

'I'm not sure he's telling us the whole truth though,' Jack replied, once they'd reached the safety of his car.

'That is for sure.'

They watched the yard as Gavin put on his full charm offensive, holding out his hand in greeting to a couple in their forties who looked like they had some disposable income to spend on a share in a racehorse. Harrison wasn't just watching Gavin, though. The stable lad, Lewis, who'd come to his office, had disappeared back inside a horsebox, but he could see him hiding in the shadows and watching them. He struck Harrison as someone who was either pathologically scared of the police or someone with something to hide. Question was, what and why?

21

Harrison sat in the car while Jack went into a Tesco store to grab some lunch. He'd just had to endure several minutes of Jack cracking jokes at his expense because Harrison had told him he'd been fasting yesterday and having eaten a big breakfast, still didn't feel like eating again. Jack's stomach had finally won the battle for his attention and he'd gone off to hunt for food.

Alone, Harrison's mind had wandered off the case to thoughts of Tanya again and how she was managing in London. He pulled his phone from his pocket and sent a text.

How are you? Any news? He was about to put the phone away until she replied, but hesitated and texted DCI Barker as well.

Any news on Tanya's stalker?

He appreciated that they both might not be able to reply quickly. Tanya could be at a crime scene, and DCI Barker said she was going to be in court a lot this week. It didn't stop him from thinking about it, though.

Jack sauntered out of the shop, munching on a large sausage roll. He flopped into the driver's seat and waved it at Harrison.

'You sure? I've got a duck wrap if you'd prefer that?'

'I'm sure.'

Jack chucked a bottle of water onto Harrison's lap and deposited the rest of his own lunch, still in the bag, on the back seat.

'So how often do you do this fasting then?' Jack asked through a mouthful of sausage roll.

'Twice a week,' Harrison replied.

'You're kidding me? What every week? That's mad. Don't you get hungry?'

'No. I'm used to it, been doing it for years.'

'What even before that doctor, what's his name… Mosley, started on it?'

'Yes.'

'I couldn't do that, I just get too hungry, I'd probably pass out or something.'

'You wouldn't. You'd just train your appetite.'

'Not sure my appetite wants training. I enjoy my food too much. Anyway, we'd better crack on. Back to the station. Got a text from DS O'Neil, they've got Richard Carter arriving in about half an hour and the DCI wants us to interview him.'

BY THE TIME they'd reached the station, Tanya had texted back to say everything was fine, and he didn't need to worry. Harrison would have liked to know exactly where the Scottish sociopath was and if the SIO in his girlfriend's murder case was on his back, but at least she was safe. He trusted DCI Barker to be on the ball, and he'd wait for her text.

'We need to talk to Craig Matlock asap once we've seen this Richard Carter,' said Jack. 'They've had to let him go without charge, but they didn't get much out of him.'

'Agreed,' Harrison replied. 'He's someone we know for sure is connected to The Horsemen and the barn.'

On their way into the station, Harrison saw Mark James walking across the car park with a colleague. He didn't look happy. His gait was slow and without energy, and he stared at the ground, not engaging with the woman he accompanied. Definitely not the man he'd seen Saturday on the

Fens. The DS didn't see him, and he thought it was probably best that he hadn't. Last thing Harrison wanted was to get caught in the middle of two sparring detective sergeants, he'd leave that one for DCI Whittaker to deal with.

TEN MINUTES LATER, another man who didn't look too happy was Jack. DS O'Neil delighted in telling them that Richard Carter had unfortunately been detained at his stables and could they go there to interview him instead.

'Do you get the impression he's trying to keep us away from the investigation?' Jack asked Harrison.

'I think that's a distinct possibility,' he replied. 'I also think they're getting ready to make an arrest and he wants us out the way.'

'What makes you think they're going to make an arrest?'

'When we walked in, DS O'Neil quickly covered over some papers on his desk. One of them was a search warrant, today's date.'

Jack sighed. 'Great to feel a part of this investigation. Who's your money on?'

'My guess would be Alex Michaels. He was publicly seen arguing and there's a rift.'

'It could be him. I'd certainly want to

interview Mr Michaels from what we've heard, but unless O'Neil is holding back on us, I can't see he has enough evidence to arrest anyone right now.'

'No, he's showing his inexperience and is too eager to impress.'

'Hey ho, let's crack-on anyways.'

Before he turned the engine on, Jack checked his mobile. He realised he'd done it several times throughout the day already and that it was out of habit. There were no missed calls from Marie, or text messages. At home, he'd have been worried about that and called her straight away. It was a great feeling to be able to pocket his phone and get on with his job, knowing she and Daniel were safe and happy.

IT TURNED out Richard Carter's dog was in the middle of giving birth and he hadn't wanted to leave her.

'Vet reckons there's five or six and she's only just got going,' he said to them both. They were standing in the kitchen of his house, looking at a barrel shaped chocolate Labrador, who was lying in her bed while her stomach rippled and moved with contractions and squirming pups. Richard's wife was sitting by her side, stroking and soothing her.

'Let's get this done,' he said to Harrison and Jack, and tipped his head for them to follow him into the other room. 'Call me if you need me, Anna,' he shouted back to his wife.

'I've agreed to help with enquiries. I don't need a lawyer, do I?' was the first thing he asked when they sat around the dining room table.

'Not unless you feel you might need one,' Jack replied. 'We are literally asking a few questions relating to the murder of Paul Lester.'

'Murder,' Richard shook his head. 'I still can't believe it.'

'You obviously knew Paul well?' Jack started.

'Yes, of course. He'd been riding for me a few years now and rented our cottage. He was a good lad. An excellent rider and he didn't deserve this.'

'Do you know anyone who might have wanted to harm him? Anyone who might bear a grudge against Paul?'

'I assume you've spoken to Gabby. Poor kid's devastated. She would have told you about the run in with Alex Michaels. We all saw it. I'm not letting him near my horses.'

'Yes, she did. Do you think the argument might have continued?'

'I think Alex was as jealous as hell about Paul's

success. He was never going to suddenly become best buddies with him.'

'Anyone else?'

Richard shook his head. 'Not that I can think of, no.'

'Did you know about The Horsemen, the secret society Paul belonged to?'

'Yeah, sure. A few of us knew it existed, but that was it. No details.'

'Were you a member Mr Carter?'

'Me? No, absolutely not. Never invited. I got the impression it was younger members. If I kept disappearing off for clandestine meetings in the evenings, I think Anna might wonder what I was up to and think I was having an affair.' He smiled.

'Anyone else here at the stables who might have been a member?'

'Not that I'm aware of. Mark Jones is one of our more experienced jockeys, along with Gabby. They'd take any big rides that Paul couldn't do, but I don't think Mark was a member. Like I say though, it was secret. They really did keep it pretty quiet so I might not know.'

'So, both Mark and Gabby rode if Paul was unavailable?'

'Yeah. He was in demand. They're both good jockeys.'

'I bet that must have been frustrating for them,' Jack prompted.

'If you're asking would Mark or, heaven forbid, Gabby, have killed Paul, then the answer is no. Sure they lost out to him for some good horses, but that's the nature of the game right? Not something you'd kill over.'

Jack didn't reply. He'd been introduced to more than enough corpses for reasons which were a lot more trivial than career rivalry.

'What about anyone who might have perhaps been a bit in awe of Paul and wanted to join The Horsemen?' Harrison asked.

Richard shook his head again, turning his mouth down in thought.

'No, seriously. Nobody that I can think of. We're a pretty straightforward team here. I don't tolerate any politics or in-fighting, everyone gets on really well.'

'I need to ask you where you were on Friday evening, Mr Carter.' Jack looked directly at him.

'You're not suggesting I'm a suspect, I hope. I was here, with my wife. You can go and ask her now if you like.'

'It's routine, but I also have to ask you about the conviction for assault when you were twenty. What were the circumstances surrounding that, please?'

'Oh Christ, are you serious? That was twenty years ago, and it was a trumped-up charge because the son of a local lawyer had attacked me and my friends and I'd given him a hiding. It was self-defence, but of course his lawyer daddy had some expensive colleagues to call on and I just had a duty solicitor who was indifferent to say the least. If you think that means I could have murdered Paul, then you're barking up the wrong tree, DS Salter. Talking of which, I should be with my dog. Are we done here?'

The indignation was plastered across Richard's face.

'Yes, thank you for your time,' Jack replied.

'Good luck with the birthing,' Harrison said to Richard as they walked out. All he got was a dismissive nod in response.

'I WONDER how many people we can manage to wind up in one day?' Jack said as they walked out the house. 'Let's have a little wander around the yard, see if anyone else here knows anything about Paul.'

They had barely walked past two horse boxes when Scott Smith's Jack Russell instincts had him cornering them like stable rats.

'Can I help you?' he asked.

'We were just looking around,' Jack replied.

'You have to understand that this yard is home to some of the country's top racehorses. We can't let people *just look around* on their own.'

'Of course, I do apologise, Mr…?'

'Scott Smith, I'm Head Lad here.'

'DS Salter, and my colleague, Dr Lane. We're investigating the murder of Paul Lester. Did you know him well?'

'We all knew him. He lived in the cottage and rode for us.'

'Did you see anything suspicious on Friday night?'

Scott shook his head.

'You live in the staff block, don't you? That looks across to Paul's cottage?' Harrison asked.

'That's right.'

'Have you ever seen anything unusual? Anyone hanging around?'

'No. Only staff.'

'Do you know anyone who might have wanted to hurt Paul?'

Scott shrugged. 'You're better off speaking to Gabby. She knows him best.'

'OK, thank you for your time.' Jack smiled, one of his forced smiles that told Harrison he didn't think too highly of Scott Smith.

They walked back to his car, but felt the unwavering gaze of Scott on their backs.

'He's a cold fish, that one,' said Jack.

'He's very protective of Richard and the horses. I think it's his way.'

'While we wait to speak to Alex Michaels, our priority has to be Craig Matlock. Agreed?'

'Definitely.'

'Let's go pay him a visit then.'

22

Craig Matlock lived at his parents' farm adjacent to the land where the barn used for The Horsemen was situated. Theirs was an arable farm, but when Jack and Harrison drove into the yard, a young man was grooming a horse. They instantly recognised him from the incident board.

Craig looked up at them as they drove in. There was a weariness on his face and he took no interest in their arrival. The chestnut gelding he was grooming munched on a bag of hay as he rhythmically brushed his coat, sending dust and debris into the afternoon breeze. Craig's shoulders were dragged down, his soul heavy. To Harrison, he was clearly a man weighed with grief.

Jack got out the car and approached him.

'Mr Matlock? DS Jack Salter,' he said, holding out his badge for Craig to see.

'You've got to be kidding. You lot had me locked up in a cell for twenty-four hours already. Can't you leave me alone?'

'I'm not here to arrest you, Mr Matlock. We're here to find out who murdered Paul.' Jack's voice had softened. He recognised a man on the edge of an emotional abyss. 'We want to catch his killer and we think you might be able to help us.'

Craig's chin wobbled slightly before he pulled himself together.

'Give me five minutes to put Charlie away,' he replied, and threw the wooden oval brush into a bucket, unhitching the horse's rein from a metal ring on the barn wall. The pair clip clopped off into the barn and Jack could hear the horse's hooves as he covered the cobbled ground, before they went silent, and a wooden door banged.

Harrison was looking around. The farm was very different to everywhere else they'd been in the week. It was clearly heavily mechanised. A huge brand-new barn was off to the left and through an open door, he saw a large machine that looked something like a combine harvester.

Craig hadn't been what he'd expected. He was of average build and height, not the slimline stature of Paul and the other jockeys. There was a lot he wanted to ask him.

Craig sloped out of the dark barn entrance door and walked towards them.

'We can go in the kitchen. My parents are both out,' he said, and as he turned to show them the way, Harrison spotted the leather thong around his neck.

'That a toad bone?' he asked him, nodding at his throat area.

Craig's face hardened and his hand went up protectively to the object hidden underneath his sweatshirt.

'That's not against the law, is it?' he asked defensively.

'Not at all. I find it interesting.' They had walked into a house that was clearly well organised and maintained. The kitchen was a combination of modern and traditional. The style was of a classic British farmhouse kitchen, but the appliances were all new and efficient. Surfaces were clutter free except for a top of the range coffeemaker, and the table was obviously not new, its top a thick slab of wood, gouged and stained with decades of family use; but it was the range that dominated the room and emitted a constant, gentle heat, which ensured a warm welcome. Craig on the other hand, was either not in the mood to be hospitable, or was purposefully not wanting them to feel welcome, because he just slumped into one of the chairs at the table and didn't ask them if they wanted a drink, or to sit down. They couldn't really blame him after his experience with their colleagues in the last 48 hours. They took his lead and sat at the table.

'I know you think I'm involved somehow, but I'm not. He was my friend. I'd never hurt him, and if I knew who did, I'd tell you.'

'As I said, Mr Matlock, we are here because we think you can shed some light on matters which could lead us to Paul's killer. We're not here to arrest you. We need you to be totally honest with us because that's the only way we're going to solve this.'

'I have been honest. I told them the truth.'

'But you didn't tell them everything though, did you?' Jack challenged.

Craig looked away from them both, staring vacantly at the kitchen Aga range, which was a dusky violet colour.

'Are you protecting someone, Craig?' Jack asked.

Craig scowled and shook his head. 'No. I said, if I knew who'd done it, I'd tell you.'

'Can you tell us about The Horsemen then,

when did the group start and who are the members?'

'It's got nothing to do with why Paul was killed.'

'He was murdered in your barn. In the place where you hold your meetings,' Jack countered.

'Yes, but it wasn't one of us. I know it wasn't.'

'You know? How can you be so sure, Craig? You said you didn't know who did it. Why not tell us who the members are and let us speak to them to be sure? They may know something you don't.'

Craig shook his head. 'Whole point of the group is that it's secret. We swear an oath.'

'I think your cover has been blown, don't you?'

Craig's lips rolled inwards. The suggestion clearly annoyed him, and he crossed his arms.

'By not identifying the DNA of those who should have been there, you might be protecting the killer. We're trying to sift through it all. It would really help our investigation if we could identify individuals now.'

Craig said nothing.

'Craig are you being threatened by someone? Did Paul or the group have links to any organised crime gangs?'

That question succeeded in only deepening Craig's scowl.

The conversation was going round in circles,

and Harrison could see his body language was getting more and more defensive.

‘Craig, are you not telling us because you think you’re honouring Paul by keeping it secret?’

Craig looked at him. Harrison could see his mind thinking through what he’d just asked.

‘Paul loved the group. His grandfather and great grandfather had been Horsemen. He inherited their book of notes and he really believed in it as a collective of those who cared for horses. It was a friendship group. Gave us a sense of purpose. There was nothing sinister.’

‘I can believe that, but I’m not sure everyone does. While everything we’ve heard about Paul says that he was a good man who looked after his horses well, somebody didn’t feel the same way. By keeping this secret, you could be protecting the killer’s identity.’

‘I’ve told you that nobody in the group could have done it.’ Craig scowled. He was getting annoyed now.

‘That might be true, but one key to finding Paul’s killer is to know how you sent the invites, the summons to meet up. I know it was a horse tail hair in an envelope, but what was the method exactly? If it wasn’t somebody from your group who murdered Paul, then it was someone else who knew how you operated. He got an envelope with a horse tail hair in it on the day he died. It's why he was at the barn to meet his murderer. Who would have access to that information?'

Craig visibly paled. 'So they used The Horsemen to get at him.' He paused, the words sinking in. 'I mean it's not common knowledge, but you can find out in books and stuff about the tradition of sending the horse's tail.'

'Talk us through the process, exactly. What kind of envelope do you use? How you communicated the date and time.'

'It was a particular type of envelope. When each man joined, he was given twenty-four of them. There's just over a dozen of us in the association and if you needed the group's help then you could summon it by sending a horse tail hair in one of the envelopes with a note inside saying the date and time for the meeting.'

'A note inside?' questioned Harrison.

'Yes.'

'Was it always a note inside, or had anyone ever deviated from that?'

'Always a note inside. I know people may laugh at our rituals, but we had strict rules and ways of doing things. When you joined, you signed up to abide by those rules.'

'And how were those envelopes delivered?'

'By hand. All the members are within a thirty-mile radius of here. Usually, we'd give people a week's notice unless it was something really urgent.'

'And no other members of the group received an invite for Friday night?'

'No.'

'Could you show us one of the envelopes, please?'

'OK.' Craig disappeared into the depths of the house, and they heard his feet tramp upstairs.

Jack turned to Harrison.

'I haven't seen the envelope Paul received, but I'm taking it that it wasn't as he'd described?'

'Nope. Plain white cheap envelope with the time written on the front. It's someone who knew the method, but not the execution well enough.'

'Or someone from the group trying to cover their tracks.'

'Maybe, but I don't think so.'

Harrison looked around the kitchen. There was one photograph on the wall of a younger Craig on a racehorse, beaming. Beside him, on another mount, was Paul who had reached out to pat his friend on the back. Harrison always felt a sadness for lives taken early, especially when they'd been much loved and missed. He didn't think he would ever get over that feeling, despite everything he saw each day. In fact, he hoped he would never get over it.

Craig's feet thumping down the stairs heralded his return.

'Here,' he said, thrusting a cream-coloured envelope at Harrison.

Harrison looked. It was completely different to the one he'd seen on Paul's bed Saturday morning. This envelope was good quality, thick cream paper and square. More like an expensive greeting card envelope than the thin white standard letter sized one with a scrawled *3 p.m.* on its exterior.

'This is clearly different from the one Paul received,' Harrison confirmed.

'Mind if we hang on to this, please?' Jack asked, reaching for the envelope.

Craig shrugged.

'Why do you think Paul didn't query it?' Jack asked him.

'What do you mean?' Craig replied.

'You know, the envelope. If it was so different, why did he just go along with it and not call someone up and say, *hey what's with the envelope, why haven't you followed protocol*?'

'I don't know. Maybe he thought one of us was in trouble. That it had been done in haste. He'd never have thought in a million years that someone would be luring him there to hurt him.

People were aware of the group, but we thought where we met and all the detail, was secret. If he thought one of us needed help, he'd have come whatever.'

'Tell us about the group Craig, what is it about?'

Craig looked up at the photograph of Paul and him on the wall.

'It was like in the old days, a kind of support group, I guess. We helped each other out whenever we could. There's a bond between us. You know if one of us needed help with getting a job or had a problem with a horse, then we'd do what we could. All of us work with horses in different ways.'

'A bit like a horsey Freemasons?' Jack asked.

Craig sneered and shrugged.

'Paul loved horses, and he'd have done anything for any one of us. That's why I know The Horsemen had nothing to do with this.'

There were a few moment's silence in the kitchen while all three thought about the man who'd been murdered.

'What did you all do with the envelopes after you'd received them?' asked Harrison.

'Burnt them, it was part of the rules.'

'And the toad bones, do you all have one?'

'Yeah, once a member was inducted into the

group, we taught them the old ways, the things that Paul's great grand pa would have done.'

'How did you know Paul?'

'We met learning to ride together. Both wanted to be jockeys. I tried, but as you can see, I wasn't really the build for it. Paul went on to be successful, and we remained really good friends.'

'Were you aware of anyone who was obsessed with Paul, or The Horsemen? Perhaps someone who wanted to join, but was refused?'

'I don't think so, no. He wasn't always popular with some people because he stood up for horses, he couldn't stand people not treating them right.'

'What about Gabby, Paul's girlfriend?'

'Oh yeah, she wanted to join, and Paul told her she couldn't. She got quite annoyed about it. Kept telling him that women had equal rights as jockeys and were as good as men, and that he was being sexist not letting her join.'

'How did Paul take that?'

'He ignored it mostly, but he wasn't going to budge on the rules. He just avoided her for a week or so and she'd usually calm down.'

'Had they argued about it recently?'

'Not sure. She's quite a fiery one, you know redheads and all that. I don't think Paul was planning long term like she was.'

'Do you think he was going to dump her?'

'Oh I don't know about that. He talked about it occasionally, usually after they'd argued. Nothing specific.'

'What about Mark Jones, who also works at Three Oaks?'

Craig shrugged and thought for a moment.

'Paul never really mentioned him much.'

'Do you understand we need to know who was in the group, Craig? Nobody's in trouble, but it could be somebody connected to them, someone who knew what went on. That includes people you might know. We believe the killer would watch your meetings through a hole that has been hidden in the barn wall. Were you aware of a hole?'

Craig's face told them he very clearly wasn't.

'No. Where? I've never noticed a hole.'

Harrison nodded and watched as the realisation dawned on Craig's face.

'So that means…'

'They'd have seen the initiation ceremony, yes,' Harrison confirmed.

Craig swore.

Jack looked from Harrison to the shocked Craig and back again.

'Do you want to talk DS Salter through what your initiation ceremony entailed, Craig?'

Craig put his face into his palms and rubbed.

'It's the way they always used to do it. Written in the book Paul got from his grandfather. You knew that you were being invited to join the association, new members were scoped out first. They'd receive the horse tail hair in the envelope. They were told to meet up with the other members at a graveyard at midnight. It's spooky right. You're told to find a particular stone and then to stand by it and wait. You're there in the dark, all alone, bricking it because of where you are, and then suddenly a hood is thrown over your head and you're led away. Your captors declare that they're The Horsemen and you shouldn't be afraid, but even so, it's pretty frightening.

'We go by car to the barn, so the new recruit doesn't know where the association meets until they've sworn the oath. Once inside, he's surrounded by the other members, chanting. Eventually, the hood is taken off so he can see them. Paul's grandad said they used to wear horse skulls on their heads, but Paul wasn't into that, so we made wooden masks. There's the oath stick, which has a hoof on the bottom, but not a horse's hoof. It's from a goat and that's why some people think you're swearing an allegiance to the Devil. On top is a pair of horns. They're actually sheep horns, and we have an oath that we read out and the recruit has to swear allegiance. It includes the punishment of death if they break the oath.

'Then we usually have a drink and toast the new member, but the final part, that's the scariest bit. The new Horseman thinks he's done, he's in, but the group will turn on him and accuse him of being false and not living by the principles of The Horsemen, that he's a traitor. The hood is put back over his head and he's marched up the ladder to the hayloft. Up to where… to where the noose was. He's told he's going to die and go to the Devil. His hands are tied behind his back and the hood is put back over his head, before the noose is placed round his neck. We do some chanting and he's pushed off the top. Only, we've untied the rope from the ring, he just falls into the hay beneath, and he's fine.'

'A fake hanging,' said Jack out loud after listening intently to Craig's story.

He nodded.

'So whoever was peering through that hole would have seen it all.'

'Or would they?' said Harrison. 'Would they have seen it *all*?'

23

Craig Matlock finally agreed that it was in the best interests of finding Paul's killer, that he told Jack and Harrison who else was in the group.

After they'd left Craig sitting at his kitchen table, mourning his friend, Jack and Harrison looked over the names in the car.

'None of these have been mentioned in the enquiry before,' Jack noted.

'No.'

'We should send this list in to the enquiry team and get it logged.'

'We should,' Harrison agreed, but looked up at Jack to see if he could detect what the hidden thoughts were in his words.

'But, seeing as DS O'Neil seems so keen to keep us out of the way of his enquiry, I think it's probably best that we don't bother him with these just yet, don't you?' Jack smirked.

Harrison smiled back.

'We're going to have to speak to all of them as quickly as possible though.' Jack sighed. 'Starting with the closest.'

First on their list was Oliver Carmichael. He was Head Lad at a racing stables just a couple of miles from where Paul had lived. They arrived mid afternoon when the stables were at their quietest, which worked out well. Oliver was in the yard office sorting out feed bills.

'That was quick,' he said as soon as they walked through the door. 'Craig said you'd be calling round, but didn't expect you so soon. Take a seat.'

It was nice to have a slightly more welcoming reception than they'd had the rest of the day. Harrison appraised the room and the man. Organised, professional, and popular, if the '*World's Greatest Boss*' mug, and clear desktop, were anything to go by.

'Fancy a brew?' he asked, gesticulating at the kettle on the side.

'I'd love a cup please, cheers,' said Jack, who was suffering from the earlier lack of beverages.

Oliver raised an eyebrow in question to Harrison.

'Just a glass of water, please,' he replied.

'No problem, I'll give you the posh mug and glass, the one we save for clients.'

While the kettle boiled, Jack got started on the interview.

'How long had you known Paul Lester?'

At the mention of his friend's name, Oliver looked noticeably less cheerful.

'He was a good mate. We met about six years ago, used to see him at races and out on the gallops. He rode a few horses for us too, but we used to meet up in town for a drink. I don't understand why anyone would want to kill him. He annoyed a few who were less than ethical in the racing world, but the vast majority of people really liked him.'

'Unfortunately, it only takes one,' said Jack as he watched Oliver pour the boiling water into his mug.

He held up a milk carton.

'Just a little, thank you.'

Harrison already had his water and was sitting listening to the conversation, but his mind was elsewhere. He was thinking back to when he'd peered through the hole in the barn wall, trying to remember the exact line of vision.

'What about your fellow Horsemen?' Jack questioned.

Oliver handed him the mug of tea and went to sit back down.

'I can promise you that none of them would have hurt Paul. There was no reason to. We are all mates.'

'I have to ask where you were on Friday night.'

'That's OK, I was in the Five Bells at Burwell. Met my girlfriend for dinner and went back to hers for a few hours before coming back to the yard. We have early starts.'

'Could I have her name?'

'Sure, Lucy Bond. She works in Newmarket for an accountant.'

'Do you keep up with any of the other members of The Horsemen outside of your meetings?'

'Yeah course, I see all of them at different times. Usually not all together. Was supposed to meet up with Sam yesterday, but he didn't show. I'm assuming he's had to deliver a horse urgently. He does transport. Helps ship horses around the country and even abroad.'

'That's Sam Brown?'

'Yeah.'

'Is there anyone you can think of who maybe wanted to join your group but couldn't, or who had a grudge to bear against Paul?'

'No. Like I said, most people liked him. I'm

sure you know he and Alex Michaels don't see eye to eye, but he's just a prat. I don't think he'd have it in him to kill someone. Wouldn't have the balls.'

'Can I ask what you do with the invitations after they've arrived?' Harrison asked.

'Burn it straight away,' said Oliver.

'And you didn't receive an invite last Friday?' Jack asked.

'No.'

'Is there anyone who could have access to your post, to have seen the invites arrive?'

Oliver thought for a moment, and slowly shook his head.

'Not really, no. They get delivered straight to our home addresses, so it's not like someone here would see it. I live on my own.'

'YOU WERE UNUSUALLY QUIET IN THERE,' Jack said to Harrison as they left. 'And that's saying something bearing in mind you're not exactly Mr Chatty at the best of times.'

'You asked the questions fine,' Harrison replied.

'What's up?' Jack stopped and looked at him.

'Two things. I think we should put Sam Brown at the top of our list for who to see next. What if this isn't just about Paul? What if it's about The

Horsemen? There could be more of them in danger. And second, I need to go back to the barn and test a theory asap.'

'OK. I'll call into the incident room and let them know we need to get back in there. Sam's not far from here. He's got a place where he stores his horse trucks, and Craig reckons he lives in a flat on site.'

JACK JUMPED into the car after his phone call to the incident room, his face animated with anger.

'You're not going to believe it. They've arrested Alex Michaels and O'Neil wants us in there now to start the interview.'

Harrison sighed heavily.

'He's convinced its him.'

'What evidence has he got?'

'Apparently it's based on his and Paul's public argument and Alex not having an alibi for Friday night.'

'We haven't met him yet, but from what everyone else says, he doesn't fit the profile. We really need to check why Sam Brown isn't answering his phone calls.'

'Agreed. Let's head to Sam's and see if there's any sign of him or where he's gone first. They're going to need to process Michaels before we can get in to see him, anyway.'

'Sam's Yard' was a small light industrial area near to the Fens. The big steel gates were unlocked and open, so they were able to drive through and park up next to a huge horse transporter. It was a sleek silver truck which looked like it was going to be just as luxurious on the inside.

'That's a beast and a half,' said Jack. 'Probably cost as much as my house.'

There were four other trucks parked alongside, of varying sizes and age.

'You'd think there'd be a bit more security than just CCTV, wouldn't you,' Jack said nodding at the cameras along the building edge.

'I think you'll find that he parks them inside at night.' Harrison looked towards the large metal structure at the other end, which reminded him of a small aircraft hangar.

'So why they not parked in there if he's gone away?' Jack said. 'And why were the gates unlocked? He must be here.'

The two men headed straight for the sign which said, 'Office'.

Jack knocked but didn't wait for a reply. He tried the door handle. It was unlocked, so he pushed the door straight open and stepped inside. As his right foot slipped and his leg nearly went under him, Harrison grabbed his arm to keep him upright. Jack didn't need to look down to know what it was he'd slipped on. The smell of death and blood filled the cramped office. Lying flat on his back in front of them, with a hole where his heart should be, was Sam Brown, surrounded by a congealed pool of his own blood. On his torso was a crucifix, and over both wrists and ankles were iron horseshoes.

'Shit!' was all Jack could say.

24

DCI Whittaker arrived on the scene just as Dr Marcus Marshall, the pathologist, carefully stepped out from Sam Brown's office. Behind him the small room was lit up with forensic lamps and two white overall'd officers were photographing and collecting evidence. In front of him, Jack, Harrison, and DS O'Neil had been waiting impatiently for his first impressions. O'Neil stood apart from them, he'd barely spoken a word to either of them since he'd arrived, he was angry that they'd ruined his moment of glory in arresting Alex Michaels, and completely ignored his request to go back to the station to interview him. Now he stood, leaning against his car, arms and eyebrows crossed defensively.

'OK, this one was stabbed before his heart

was cut out.' Dr Marshall addressed his waiting audience. 'Several puncture wounds in his back, at least one of which would have perforated a lung.'

'We've a suspect in custody, so what we need to know is an estimated time of death,' DS O'Neil said to him.

Harrison could hear the hope in his voice and see the DS was nervous. He'd obviously managed to convince most of the team that Alex was their man, but as he'd been up in Doncaster for the past two days, with TV footage of him racing, as well as hundreds of eyewitnesses, the timing was going to be critical.

'I'd say a little over twenty-four hours, but not as much as forty-eight,' Dr Marshall replied.

'From what you've seen, does the way the heart's been cut out look like the same killer as Paul Lester?' Jack asked. 'It's a different cause of death, so it might not be the same man.'

'Well, obviously I need to get him into my lab and look at the wound in detail, but from what I've seen so far, the modus operandi looks the same. No finesse or training, he's just gone straight in there and wrenched it out, cutting whatever was necessary. Same as for Paul.'

Jack was secretly enjoying the look on DS O'Neil's face. After he'd clearly tried to get one over on them, he'd been hoping for a chance to get one back. They'd found another victim, changed the focus of the case, and proved that DS O'Neil's hasty conclusions were wrong.

'You'd better get back and let Michaels out for now,' DCI Whittaker said to O'Neil. 'Get a statement and then let him go.'

'Yes, boss,' the DS replied, and stomped back to his car without even a glance in Jack's or Harrison's direction.

'So, DS Salter and Dr Lane, any thoughts?'

'First thing is to warn the other members of The Horsemen that they need to take extra precautions. The killer could strike again,' Jack said.

'Agreed, I'll get uniforms out to all the addresses you've given us.'

'Dr Lane, anything that's standing out to you?'

'I have a theory for the motive, but I need to get back to the barn to confirm it.'

'I won't hold you up. Forensics have this scene under control. You do what you need to and don't forget if there's anything I can do to help, just let me know.'

JACK WAS SITTING in the car outside the DIY store waiting for Harrison to reappear. He'd muttered that he needed to get something and disappeared into the shop without any further explanation. The smell of death was still in Jack's nostrils and he sat with the windows open, preferring the chill to being reminded about what he'd recently stepped in. He texted Marie to see how things were going at her parents. She replied almost straight away:

Sitting watching mum photographing dad holding Daniel. She's taken about fifty photos already!!!

He was still beaming when Harrison yanked open the back passenger door and flung in a length of rope before sitting back down beside him in the front.

'Just had a text from Marie. She's had a great day.' Jack said to him. 'I'm actually looking forward to getting back to them now.'

'This won't take long,' Harrison said to him reassuringly.

Jack started the engine and headed towards the barn.

'So why do you think he stabbed Sam but hung Paul?' Jack was thinking out loud in the car.

'Sam was a big bloke. He could have easily overpowered the man who took Paul's body to the Fen. The only hope he would have had to kill him was the element of surprise, hence knife in the back.'

'So he could have known his killer, else why

would you turn your back on someone who you weren't sure about.'

'Possibly. The horse racing world is a small one. If they're in it, which chances are they are, then they'll know a lot of people,' replied Harrison.

They were both tired by now. It had been a long day and the surge of adrenalin that came with discovering the latest victim had slumped and was slowing them down.

'What is it you need to do at the barn?' Jack asked.

'When I looked through the hole, I was viewing what I already knew to be there. What if the killer saw something different?'

Jack sighed.

'OK. Sometimes you talk in riddles, but I'm sure it will become crystal clear when we get there.'

'Indeed,' replied Harrison.

They let the mind-numbing sound of car tyre on road fill their heads for the remainder of the journey, trying to blank out the image of Sam Brown from their minds.

By the time they reached the barn, it had gone 7 p.m.

'I need you to come into the barn with me.'

Harrison said to Jack, grabbing the rope from the rear seat.

A uniformed police officer was sitting in a car waiting for them. He had the key to the big padlock on the barn door, there to prevent anyone from going in and either contaminating evidence or going on some gruesome treasure hunt. There were times the police couldn't believe some of the selfies that appeared on Instagram or one of the true crime sites following a murder.

Once inside, Harrison led Jack up the ladder to the hayloft, and over to where he believed the hangman's noose had been tied.

'I'm going to put this into the position I think the original noose would have been,' he said, hurling the rope above him so that it wrapped over once on the big beam above. As the other end swung towards them, he caught it. 'I need something to tie to the end. Attach this end to the ring and hold onto the other, would you?'

Harrison went back down the ladder to where the forensics officers had earlier been collecting up all the hay. They were all done. A stack of bags sat piled in place of the large loose hay mound. He took one of the bags and carried it back up to where Jack stood waiting, with a quizzical look on his face, and then tied the rope around the neck of the bag.

'It's not ideal, too short, but it will give me an idea.'

Jack just watched him and did as he was told. He hadn't a clue what Harrison was up to, but he knew there would be a reason behind it, and so he went along with it.

'I'm going to go outside and look through the hole. When I bang the side of the barn wall, I need you to untie the end of the noose from the ring and push the hay bundle and noose off the side.'

'So the whole rope and the bag falls?' Jack clarified.

'Yes.'

'OK, got it.'

'Stay standing there too, would you, but don't fall off. The hay's gone now.'

Jack looked at Harrison. Was that an attempt at humour, or him being serious? He couldn't tell. Harrison was already on his way back down the ladder.

Once outside, Harrison picked his way around the side of the barn to where he could see the light coming through the hole. It was easy in the dark now that they had taken the plug away for analysis. The hole was at Harrison's upper chest height, the same height as he'd estimated the man on the Fen to be. He bent his knees and crouched down. It was essential that he got the same angle of view as the peeping Tom would have got. In front of him, he saw the area where the ceremony would have taken place, but the spot where the hay had once sat wasn't visible. The wooden backed pews and the straw bales severely restricted the view on the ground. He could see Jack and the bag of hay, on the edge of the hayloft, but only just. The central pillar of the barn rose up and blocked most of the view. Harrison moved around, trying to see if he could see more, but it was impossible, whatever angle he tried.

He banged his hand flat on the side of the barn loudly and saw Jack respond. He watched the movement as Jack pushed the bag of hay from the top and briefly saw the bag and the noose plunge over the edge, before they disappeared again behind the pillar. That was it. That's all the killer would have seen of the mock execution. There was no other viewpoint, no way to have seen the newly initiated recruit land in the bed of hay, or the rope come falling down with him.

Jack started climbing down the ladder, and so Harrison went to meet him at the barn door entrance.

'Well?' Jack asked.

'They couldn't see that it was fake. From their

viewpoint you could have watched The Horsemen swear their allegiance on a staff that looked like it was meant for the devil. Then they'd have seen the recruit taken up the ladder, blindfolded, and pushed off the top with a noose around his neck. What they couldn't see was the rope fall down with him, or the man land in the hay. What they would have seen next was that man up and walking, probably laughing with relief, as though he were back from the dead. To them, The Horsemen are the Devil's revenants and they're trying to kill the undead.'

25

Harrison returned to his hotel room and went straight to the shower to wash off the day's death and crime. He was exhausted, eyes tired and head aching from the events of the day. His stomach felt hollowed and empty, but it wasn't complaining. He hadn't felt hunger cravings in a long time, his body used to the more natural rhythm of eating and fasting that our ancestors would have followed. Tonight, he would order room service. He couldn't face making an effort to get dressed again and then have to talk to strangers.

It felt good lying on the bed in the quiet. The hotel wasn't full, and he heard only the occasional bang of a door from further down the corridor, or the swish, swish, of someone walking past his room. They'd only been in Cambridgeshire a day, but he was pleased with their progress. There was also a sadness. Had the investigation been handled differently right from the start, perhaps Sam Brown would still be alive.

He checked through his emails. Ryan had been in touch to say he might be on the track of someone who'd witnessed the murder at Nunhead Cemetery in 1993, and that Harrison had also been called by Leo Fawcett from the National Crime Agency who didn't leave a number but said he'd call back.

There were a couple of requests from other investigation teams at the Met who'd found unusual objects at crime scenes. The first one was simple. It was a brown shrivelled hand, which he immediately recognised as being a stolen relic of a mummified Saint. The second request took slightly longer as an inscription had been found in the room where a prostitute had been murdered. The seriousness of the case and the implications of the inscription warranted a longer email.

The woman's murder had made the news, but not the front pages. It was a sad and disturbing truth that an attack on a prostitute was not seen to be as serious by the newspaper buying public, and therefore journalists who wrote the stories, as a young woman walking home after a night out. Sex workers were second-class citizens relegated to side columns, and like homeless people, they made easier victims. Most didn't have the family support to push for justice, or in some cases, even have it noticed that they'd disappeared. To Harrison they were still human beings who deserved justice and as much of his time as he'd give to a middle-class professional woman.

In this particular enquiry, he was also concerned that the killer might not just be a one-off attacker. There was anger evident in the murder, and in the words he'd scrawled on the unfortunate woman's wall. Harrison only needed to read the first few words to know what it was:

*Coraxo cahisa coremepe, od belanusa Lucal*a…

It was a long paragraph, an Enochian key, a call out to Satan in his language. This particular one, the tenth, was designed to create anger and violence. Whoever wrote it had probably found it in a copy of *The Satanic Bible* by Antony LaVey. Harrison doubted he'd have taken the book to the crime scene, so he must have memorised the words. Even the way he'd written it on the wall, with hard pressure used, especially in the downward strokes and a straight right slant on the starting letters, showed anger. This was a man dangerously out of control.

He conveyed his fears to the detective on the

case, confirming their suspicions that the man would have been building up to the killing, so they should look for someone who liked violent sex and had probably overstepped the mark more than once. The sex workers needed to be careful, he'd do it again and would have been emboldened by the surge in adrenaline and pleasure he'd got so wouldn't take long to seek out his next victim. If he wasn't caught, it wouldn't be long before he might graduate from the easy targets and start on the general population. Then the papers would take notice.

Harrison asked the detective to send over some more photographs of the crime scene, because it might help him build a better profile of the killer for them. The victim's eyes had been covered for one thing, and there were other indicators which Harrison thought might show a complex relationship with a female figure, possibly his mother, or maybe a wife.

Reading emails like that didn't help Harrison relax for sleep. It made him both sad and angry for the victims. For a while, he lay on the bed thinking about the fact that out there right now, someone was being attacked. Then he thought about Tanya, and that made things worse. DCI Barker had been in touch to say that all was quiet. The SIO on the other case was on-board and taking their information seriously. There was a review of the investigation underway, and they were expecting to re-interview the sociopath boyfriend tomorrow. It was good to know Sandra was on top of it, but he'd still rather be in London close to Tanya, just in case.

Room service arrived with a quick knock on the door. The young lad who brought it clearly took pride in his work. He was African, dressed immaculately in his hotel uniform, and handed Harrison's dinner over with a huge smile. He tipped him a couple of pounds and thanked him. Just those few seconds of pleasantness with another human being, had taken the edge off the darker thoughts in his head.

Harrison had opted for a club sandwich with fries, and surprised himself at how quickly the whole lot disappeared. Perhaps he'd been hungry after all.

Food eaten, Harrison resorted to turning on some music to take his mind off reality. At times like this, when his head was full of the violence of the day, it was difficult to meditate and go to a more peaceful place in his conscience. The music gave him a rhythm to relax to, lyrics to concentrate on, and thankfully he was so tired that he was asleep within half an hour.

. . .

Jack arrived at his in-laws to find they'd waited for his return before having dinner. Daniel, appeared to have been totally worn out by the day's cuddling and photographic shoots, because he'd been fed and put to bed and they'd not heard a peep out of him. Marie was sitting on the sofa, relaxed and smiling. Jack walked into the sitting room to find her chatting with her parents, a glass of wine in hand. The scene had brought an instant smile to his face.

Marie's parents weren't well off, but like most working people of their age, they'd saved and had pensions and so there was a nice nest egg to add to their home, which they'd bought at a fraction of today's prices, back in the 1980s. The house was a semi-detached with slightly outdated decor, but comfortable. In the rear was a mature garden where in summer her parents would sit under the overhang and have breakfast most mornings, and watch the birds. It was the home that Marie had been brought up in. An ex council property purchased at a massively reduced rate thanks to Margaret Thatcher's right to buy policy to encourage home ownership. Every room was filled with warm memories of her childhood, and Jack felt that warmth wrapped around her and in the smile on her face.

He'd always got on fine with her parents, but

sitting around the dinner table, talking about Daniel, Marie as a baby, and all the other every day family talk, had made Jack appreciate them more than he'd ever thought possible. Not only were they a total antidote to the day job, but they'd helped his wife smile again. There was a light in Marie's eyes, which he hadn't seen in months. The girl he'd married was starting to come back to him after months of post-natal depression, worry, and stress. He wondered if her parents had noticed it. If Marie's mother saw the haunted look in her eyes, or the flicker of fear when she looked at Daniel. Tonight, it was gone. He knew that there would still be difficult times ahead, but this was a huge step forward for them, and as Jack tucked into an extra helping of Beef Stroganoff, he felt the warmth of his family all around him.

26

In the morning, Harrison didn't bother with breakfast. He was too eager to get going, and was up and on his bike heading for the station for an 8 a.m. arrival.

The incident room was fairly quiet when he arrived, last night's long hours evident in the debris that two cleaning staff were attempting to clear away. There was no sign of DS O'Neil, but the incident board had been updated. Alex Michaels was no longer the chief suspect, although the names of the other Horsemen had been added as persons of interest. Harrison doubted any of them were to blame, but knew every possibility had to be checked out.

He logged on to the system and looked through the material that the rest of the team had gathered, including the interviews with other friends and family. The big hope had been that Sam's CCTV might have caught his killer, but whoever it was, wasn't daft. They'd gone in and erased all the recordings and although the team were looking to see if there was any way they could be retrieved, it wasn't looking hopeful.

Sam was in with Dr Marshall later that morning, so they'd get confirmation around lunchtime that it was the same killer.

A telephone rang behind Harrison and an officer answered it. He could just hear what was being said above the whine of the hoover which had now been dragged into the DCI's office.

'DS O'Neill's phone. No, OK. Great, I will, thank you.'

Harrison was typing up some notes from yesterday when he heard footsteps behind him, and a young detective appeared at his side. It was the same officer who had connected the barn in Felton Woods with their murder scene.

'Doctor Lane?' he said.

'Yes,'

'That was the forensic lab. They found a DNA match on the horsehair and envelope which was at Paul Lester's house.'

Harrison was suddenly very interested. The young officer consulted his notes.

'It's a Gavin Eamonn Simons, arrested in 2005 for being drunk and disorderly. It's a good match, a one in a billion chance that it's not him.'

By the time Jack arrived, looking well rested, a warrant to search Gavin Simon's property had already been obtained, and a team was on its way to make the arrest.

'So, it's like Gabby said then,' Jack looked at Harrison. 'Why are you not looking a bit more cheerful?'

Harrison was leaning back in his chair, with a frown of concentration, twirling a pen in one hand.

'I think some of it fits. But it's the same as it has been throughout this case, we somehow only seem to be getting half the picture.'

'He's got motive though right?' pressed Jack.

'Yeah, for Paul, he thinks he framed him for the ketamine. But why Sam? That doesn't add up.'

'Maybe he thinks all The Horsemen are the same and bears a grudge against them all?'

'That's some grudge.'

Jack gave a half nod in tacit agreement.

'The superstition stuff. From what we saw in his office, as well as what he said, it did look to be superficial, a marketing ploy. I need to get into his property, take a look around to really know.'

'The DCI wants us leading on the interviews. He's asked if you can brief DC Potter and I. We'll conduct it, you listen in.'

'OK, assuming he denies the murder, I want to know why he went to all the trouble of faking The Horsemen invite and getting him to the barn? Why not just knock on his door and have it out with him? Was someone else there with them? Did he hurt him in any way, even if he didn't kill him? Knock him out or something? Could he have been the manual strangler prior to the hanging?'

Jack scribbled all Harrison's advice down, along with a few other suggestions, before heading off to find DC Potter.

The three of them arrived in the custody area, just as a young officer was walking out with Gavin's mobile phone in an evidence bag. His lawyer was already in the briefing room with a totally deflated Gavin, who had his head in his hands and now and then would lift it up for just long enough to shake it.

DC Potter went to make sure the interview room was organised, while Jack and Harrison lent up against the custody suite desk, waiting for Gavin's lawyer to give them the word that they were ready. Both men were watching Gavin's body language through the glass wall of the briefing room.

The relative peace was suddenly smashed as a snarling skinhead burst through the door into the custody area from the garage. He was swearing and hurling abuse at the two young police officers who were attempting to get him inside without any of them being injured. One of the officers was black, and the prisoner was being vociferous with his unsavoury words about his colour. Harrison could see both officers were at the point where they were weighing up the damage to their careers that a swift punch would deliver.

'Need a hand, lads?' Harrison asked, standing up to his full height. He didn't look at the police officers. He reserved his gaze for the squirming skinhead in their grip, and it was a gaze that didn't mess about. The intensity of his stare and the sight of him stretching out his arms ready to help, was enough to stop the prisoner mid-sentence. If you could call it a sentence. Turned out he wasn't so tough after all.

The man stared back at Harrison as he was propelled towards the desk to be checked in. As he got closer, Harrison could see the dilated pupils and needle tracks in his arms. He was still tripping. They'd have to put him in a cell on watch until he'd sobered up enough for them to be able to charge him. A waste of police time and money, but at least he wasn't on the streets to abuse other people for a while.

The man didn't take his eyes off Harrison who continued to stare back until he'd been booked in and carted off.

'Thanks,' the young black officer said as they disappeared off to the cells with him.

The custody suite had just returned to peace and quiet when the door to the briefing room opened and Gavin's solicitor came out.

'My client is now ready to clear up this misunderstanding,' he said, starting as Gavin's defence clearly intended to go on.

Gavin wasn't the same man he'd been back on his home turf. He looked beat and avoided eye contact with both Jack and DC Potter. He said nothing until he had to confirm his name for the tape. Harrison sat in the far corner of the room, watching proceedings. Gavin clearly wasn't happy about the position he found himself in. The luck of the Irish had well and truly deserted him.

'Why don't you tell us what happened on Friday, Mr Simons,' Jack started.

'I wanted to speak to Paul, somewhere in

private because I was sure I was being tailed by a newspaper reporter after the ketamine ruling. I knew about The Horsemen, his private group. I'd read about the horsehair thing and some of the lads talked about how someone they knew had received one of the invites. All I had to do was send it, follow him, and he'd lead me to where they met. I know he fitted me up for the ketamine. He'd threatened that he was going to report me to race authorities two weeks before, but he had no evidence I'd done anything wrong. So instead, he gave one of my horses the ketamine. I'd already contacted my solicitor about it, but I wanted to confront him.'

'Why not just talk to him at his cottage?'

'Because it was his own turf. I wanted to surprise him, show I could find his so-called secret hiding place.'

'You wanted to scare him? Intimidate him?' Jack pushed.

'A little–' Gavin looked to his solicitor who had shifted uncomfortably in his seat. 'I didn't go there intending to hurt him. Just spook him.'

'Go on. You sent the invite, then what?

'I followed him from his cottage. I knew roughly what time he was going to leave so it wasn't hard.'

'What happened when you got to the barn?'

'As soon as we got close, I figured out where he was going and held back so he didn't realise I'd followed him. By the time I pulled up to the barn, he was already inside. So I went in. He was shocked, course he was, so I confronted him about the ketamine. He denied it, but I knew he wasn't telling me the truth. Now I'm not going to lie. Things did get a bit heated, and he got spooked. Ran up the ladder to the hayloft. I think his idea was to pull the ladder up so I couldn't reach him, but he wasn't strong enough and I stopped him and went up too. I had him trapped then. But I never touched him. He was begging me not to hurt him. Said it hadn't been him. I said a few words and left.'

'You left?'

'Yeah, there was no point carrying it on. He wasn't going to own up to it. I'd achieved what I wanted to do, which was to scare him. I'm no killer and I didn't want a GBH charge, so I told him I had his card marked and left. He was alive when I walked out that barn. I swear, I didn't kill him.'

'Mr Simons, are you saying that you didn't lay a finger on Paul Lester? Why would he have run away from you unless he thought you were going to hurt him?'

'I didn't kill him. He was alive when I left.'

'Did you attack Mr Lester?'

Gavin Simons looked to his solicitor.

'My client has told you what happened, DS Salter. I understand you're looking for the killer of Paul Lester, that is not my client.'

'I'm asking if Mr Simons attacked Paul Lester while at the barn?'

'I've told you what happened.'

'Did you physically attack Mr Lester in any way?'

'No comment,' Gavin said, looking defiantly at Jack.

'Did you try to strangle, Mr Lester?'

'No comment.'

'Was anyone else with you at the barn, apart from Paul?'

'No.'

'Do you know Sam Brown?'

'Sam? Yeah, we rent boxes off him occasionally, and he moves our horses around. Why?'

'Where were you between the hours of 4 p.m. on Sunday afternoon and Monday at 4 p.m.?'

'Why? What's this about?'

'Please, just answer the question, Mr Simons.'

'At a guess I'd say at the yard. I don't think I went anywhere.'

'And can anyone verify that you were there?'

'Yeah, the staff. I'll have to double check my diary, but with the race ban thanks to Paul Lester, I'm pretty grounded.'

'I need you to tell us your whereabouts in those twenty-four hours please and give us names of those who we can ask for confirmation.'

Gavin's face changed as the reason for the questions dawned on him.

'Has something happened to Sam?'

'I'm now terminating this interview. We can reconvene in a few hours after we've carried out the basic search of your property and checked your alibi. I expect to have initial results around lunchtime.'

'No, wait. Has Sam been killed?'

Jack turned off the tape recorder.

'You'll be escorted back to your cell, Mr Simons, and we'll let your solicitor know when we can reconvene this interview.'

Jack had purposely been brusque with Gavin Simons. He wanted to make him sweat, and now that he realised there could potentially be two murder charges coming his way, the stakes were even higher.

After their prisoner had been escorted back to

a cell, Harrison, Jack and DC Potter, had a quick debrief.

'So, what do you reckon?' Jack asked Harrison, 'Do you think he could have done it? Is Gavin our murderer?'

'Well, I don't think he just had a nice little chat with him, like he's trying to make out.'

'No. For sure. Five minutes with him and you can see he's studied at the school of hard knocks. I've sent Gavin's fingerprints to Dr Marshall, the pathologist, see if he can get any kind of match on the marks around Paul's neck.'

'I think we should be looking for more than one man,' Harrison said.

'But wasn't there only one set of footprints at the Fen?' DC Potter chipped in.

'Yes, there was. Only one person took Paul's body there, but I don't think that's the same person who strangled him. Fen man, or woman, wasn't big enough to have overwhelmed him, he certainly wasn't Gavin's size. Whoever tried to manually strangle Paul was quite a bit bigger than him. The person who took his body to the Fen was a little heavier than Paul, but not by much, and judging by the length of their strides and the height of the hole in the barn wall, they weren't all that tall either. All the way along something has not seemed straightforward about this, and I think that's it. What if Gavin isn't totally lying? What if he argued with Paul and tried to strangle him, then stopped himself and left him alive? Then after he'd gone, someone else—the peeping Tom—went in there and finished the job, and cut out Paul's heart? The more I've seen of this case, the more I'm convinced we're looking for two people. We've got an attacker, but the killer is still out there.'

27

Harrison, Jack and DC Potter, arrived back in the incident room, just as the first officers returned from the search of Gavin Simons' house and yard. There was a lot of chatter and joking, spirits were high with the hopes that the enquiry was starting to make some real progress. DS O'Neil was the only man in the room not looking cheerful. His face was pinched and Harrison could see the tension in his shoulders and neck. He could almost feel sorry for him if it wasn't for the fiery looks he kept throwing in his and Jack's direction.

With a good chunk of the team back at their desks, DS O'Neil called a briefing. All those who were there gathered around the incident board for an update. He led.

'DS Salter has just interviewed Gavin Simons, whose DNA was found on the invite which lured Paul to the location of his murder. Would you give us an update?'

'Sure. He's admitted that he sent the invite and followed Paul to the barn where he confronted him, but he claims that he didn't hurt him and is adamant Paul was alive when he left.'

'What evidence do we have to bring a charge?' DS O'Neil questioned.

Jack thought that was the wrong question to be asking. O'Neil seemed to be more concerned about bringing charges than he was about finding the truth—but he didn't voice that fact.

'With regard to the murder itself, nothing. I've sent his fingerprints over to pathology to take a look at the manual strangulation marks around Paul's neck. He claims he was at home at the time that Sam was killed and so we're just getting that checked out now with staff. Do we have a narrower time of death yet?'

'Yes. Dr Marshall is still in with Sam, but he's told me that he believes it's the same killer, and that estimated time of death was between midday and 6 p.m. on the Monday.'

'Simons seemed genuinely surprised at the mention of Sam's name, and Harrison thinks we should be looking for a second man in relation to the deaths.'

'Whoa, second man? But, Dr Lane, you were always adamant that there was just one man.' DS O'Neil couldn't hold back the jubilant sarcasm in his voice.

Harrison stood up from the desk he'd been leaning on in order to address O'Neil's question.

'I said that there was one man who took Paul's body to the Fen, and I believe that same man cut out his heart, and murdered Sam Brown. I think he took advantage of a situation caused by Gavin Simons, which left Paul Lester incapacitated. We've found evidence that someone has been spying on The Horsemen rituals. We know that the initiation involved various rites and culminated with a mock hanging. After viewing what that person would have seen, I believe the killer thinks members of the group are swearing an allegiance to Satan and are then being hanged. From his viewpoint, he couldn't see that the hangings were fake. All he saw was the men, in effect, coming back to life.'

'Are you telling me he thinks they're zombies?' DS O'Neil scoffed.

'Similar. Revenants, the undead. They don't eat peoples' brains.' Harrison replied matter-of-factly and without rising to O'Neil's tone.

A few of the officers sniggered at that remark, and Jack was impressed that Harrison had managed to crack a joke, although he wasn't sure it was intentional.

'OK, but why would Gavin Simons go to these great lengths to lure Paul Lester to the barn?'

Jack spoke now. He could see O'Neil was gunning for Harrison, and so he brought it back to standard police procedure.

'Paul found out that Gavin Simons is using, what he considered to be, dangerous methods to get the racehorses to perform at their best. He threatened to tell the race authorities if Simons didn't stop. Next thing Gavin knows, he's being hauled up after officials found ketamine in one of his horses. He swears that was nothing to do with him and he thinks Paul framed him. He wanted to confront him about it, and almost certainly wanted to scare the living daylights out of him so needed to do it somewhere secluded. Gavin's the type who would take an argument outside and sort it the old school way.' Jack said.

'Gavin reasoned that by humiliating Paul in a place that he thought nobody knew about, it would belittle him.' Harrison added, 'Make his secret society a mockery, invade his privacy. He'd already intimated what he thought about The Horsemen to us in a previous conversation.'

O'Neil scowled.

'Sir, I might be able to help with the ketamine,' a female detective spoke up. 'I've just come back from searching Simons' house. We had to return because we arrested one of his staff, a stable lad, for possession of ketamine. I think he's a heavy user, showing signs of bladder damage, could barely make it to the station he needed a pee so bad.'

'Sir, there was that case last year where a stable lad peed in a horse's stall after taking cocaine the day before.' One of the uniformed officers said. 'It soaked into its hay bedding, the horse ate it, and then tested positive for cocaine at its next meet. It's not just happened the once either.'

'So, Gavin Simons was probably angry at the wrong man,' DS O'Neil said, his brain finally catching up with the facts.

'I presume you didn't find the hearts?' Harrison asked the female detective. She shook her head.

'If you're right, then we're no closer to finding the killer.' DS O'Neil looked at Harrison, almost triumphantly.

'I have some ideas,' Harrison replied.

'Ideas don't make convictions. We have Gavin Simons' DNA on the invite, that's evidence he was involved somehow.'

'Yes, physical evidence can't be wrong DS O'Neil, but the interpretation of it is what leads to misunderstanding and an incorrect summation.'

'What's that mean? That you can ignore police procedure because you've got a gut feeling about something?' O'Neil was getting angry now at being challenged publicly by Harrison. He'd already got egg on his face from Alex Michaels, now the outsider from London, who wasn't even a trained police officer, was questioning him in front of his colleagues again.

Harrison saw the large vein in DS O'Neil's neck bulge and twitch as his blood pressure rose.

'No. Intuition transfers your own biases and prejudices onto the situation. It's based on your own experiences which might have no relation whatsoever to the killer's or the victim's.'

'Thanks for the psychiatry lesson, but what exactly are you trying to say here?' O'Neil planted his feet wider, a man positioning himself for confrontation.

'I'm saying that we need to put ourselves into the mind of the killer and work out why he's behaving in this way.'

'So you're going to be a shrink to an invisible man. Surely he's doing it because he wants to.

Simple. What's the point of trying to work out why he's behaving the way he is?'

'No, DS O'Neil, psychiatrists are probably the only medical experts who never actually look at the organ they're trying to treat. Cardiologists and orthopaedic doctors do, but psychiatrists can't see the root cause of a problem. It's the behaviour of somebody that leads them towards understanding what's happening inside the brain and finding the why. This man is obsessive-compulsive. He is highly suggestive to ritualistic and religious stimuli. He's scared. He probably believes he's protecting himself and those around him. Chances are there's something in his past which has created this kind of behaviour. Occasionally, but very rarely, it's because of a physical brain abnormality such as a tumour. So, you see, we can't perceive the issue. He could be standing in this room right now and you wouldn't know, but his behaviour would eventually give him away.'

'You'll be arresting one of us next then! Well, we have a police investigation to undertake.' DS O'Neil almost spat through clenched jaws, 'We don't need any more head doctor talk. Back to work everyone. What we do need is more hard evidence so that we can catch a killer, or charge the man we already have locked up.'

DS O'Neil shot a look of disdain at both Jack and Harrison before walking back to his desk.

'That went down well,' Jack muttered to Harrison. 'Maybe hold back on the psychiatry lesson next time?'

Harrison ignored his last remark.

'We need a quick word with Gavin, and then I'd like to go back to Paul's cottage. When I was last there, it was difficult for me to concentrate. That's where the trail starts.'

28

Gavin Simons didn't look overly pleased to see Harrison and Jack. He'd been lying on the metal bed—if you could call the steel shelf of the holding cell that—eyes closed and arms clasped across his chest like a mausoleum carving. As they entered his cell, he turned his head to give them a look of contempt and then resumed the same sleeping position.

'Mr Simons, we wanted to inform you about a development following the search of your property,' Jack started.

'Development?' Gavin sat up and spun his legs round to face them, seated. 'Does that mean you're letting me out? Come to your bloody senses?'

‘No Mr Simons, you are still a person of interest in our enquiry.’

Gavin growled.

‘If someone has planted evidence…’

‘It’s related to the reason you’re here,’ Jack continued. ‘And it’s connected to one of your staff.’

The angry attitude was instantly replaced with an attentive one.

‘My staff? You’re not saying one of them…’

‘Lewis Moffat has been arrested for possession of a sizeable amount of ketamine, which he said is for personal use.’

‘Lewis! Ketamine.’ Gavin’s mouth hung open.

‘We think that Lewis may have been the cause of your recent racing ban. He has issues with his bladder because of ketamine abuse, he can’t go for long periods without needing a toilet. He has admitted to relieving himself in the horse stables at times, and we think this could have then been transferred to the animal via its bedding.’

Gavin swore and jumped up from his seat, thumped the wall, and then swore again. He paced up and down the small cell before spinning back round to face the two men who had stood silently watching him.

‘So, it wasn’t Paul who drugged the horse?’

‘We can’t say that for sure, but based on what

Lewis has told my colleagues, it doesn't look likely, no.'

Gavin collapsed back onto the bed and put his head into his hands.

'All this is for nothing. I swear to you I didn't kill him,' he added.

'I have a question for you, Mr Simons,' Harrison spoke now. 'If you're telling the truth, then it will help us find the real killer.'

Gavin looked up and studied the big man in front of him.

'OK.'

'The invitation. How did you get it to Paul?'

'I took it round in the early hours of the morning and put it in the postbox.' He shrugged. 'Made sure no one saw me.'

'OK, thank you.'

Jack and Harrison turned to leave.

'What about me, what happens now?'

'I'm sure your lawyer has told you that you can be held for twenty-four hours without charge, after which we would have to apply to keep you longer, but only if there was good evidence that you were about to be charged.'

'You going to charge me with murder?'

'Mr Simons, I can't tell you that right now. We need to carry on our investigation and will be back in a couple of hours.'

Gavin Simons swore again and flounced back onto the metal bed.

'THERE'S NOT enough to charge him with murder,' Harrison said to Jack as they walked down the corridor and out of the building to the car park.

'No, but attempted assault is on the cards, for sure. Let him sweat for a bit longer. He might feel like being more honest with us once we've heard back from Dr Marshall about those finger marks.'

THE THREE OAKS Stables yard was quiet when they arrived, no signs of Scott Smith, which was a first, and so Jack and Harrison drove straight to Richard Carter's house and knocked on the front door. There was no reply. The two men listened and caught the distant murmur of voices. Harrison peered through the windows while Jack walked around the side of the house.

'They're in the garden.' He motioned to Harrison.

Down the side of the house, and into the back, where they came to a fenced off lawn area. At the end was a group of people all stood staring at the ground in front of them. Harrison strained to see what they were looking at. It was a tiny mound of earth with a small wooden cross sticking up.

The group comprised Richard, his wife, two young children, and Scott Smith. One of the little girls was reading something, while the rest stood reverently listening.

Scott saw Jack and Harrison first and nudged Richard, who raised his eyes heavenward, shook his head and, after whispering something to his family, walked over to them.

'We're sorry to intrude,' Jack said. 'We need access to Paul's cottage, and I understand you have the key?'

'I gave it to the forensics team on Sunday,' Richard replied. 'Don't you people talk to each other?'

'Our understanding was that it had been returned,' Jack replied politely, not rising to the tone in Richard's voice.

Behind them, the solemn gathering was breaking up, and the children and their mother were heading back to the house. Scott limped up alongside Richard.

'Scott, did Paul's cottage key get handed back?' he asked him.

'Yes, it did. I have it in my office, sorry that was yesterday and I'd forgotten to bring it back to the house.'

'No problem, you wouldn't mind getting it for these gentlemen, would you?' he asked.

'Of course,' Scott replied and picking up the spade that had been placed on the lawn post-grave-digging, walked off to retrieve it.

'One of the pups?' Harrison nodded towards the tiny grave at the end of the garden.

'Yes,' Richard replied a little surprised that he had worked it out. 'Unfortunately, it was born with some severe health problems. We had five healthy ones, but that little fella was going to have a lifetime of trouble and pain.'

'That must have been upsetting for the kids to see it being put to sleep then,' Jack said, thinking forward to when they might get a pet for Daniel.

'Actually, Scott dispatched it for me. I couldn't do it and was going to call the vet, but he said he'd sort it out. Then we told the kids that it had died in its sleep, so they were none the wiser.'

'Don't think I could have done that either,' Jack said grim faced. 'Not a little puppy.'

'Yes, I was surprised Scott offered. I think he must be more of a cat man. Got all upset when we found a mummified cat in the walls of the old hay barn, where we're doing the staff accommodation renovations. Never seen him so animated.'

'Really? Mummified cat?' Harrison asked.

'It was buried in the wall. Workmen said

they've found all sorts of things in old buildings. People used to put them there to ward off evil spirits apparently.'

'That's right, they did,' Harrison replied. 'What happened with the cat?'

'Well, there were various suggestions as to what to do with it. The kids wanted to bury it, I wanted to give it to a local museum, but Scott said it had to go back.'

'What's that?' Scott had come up behind them as they were talking.

'The cat we found in the walls of the old hay barn.'

'Yeah. I thought it was only right that it went back. It was a part of the history of that building,' Scott replied, throwing a glance at Harrison. 'Here's the key to Paul's.' He dropped it into Jack's palm.

Jack could barely keep up with Harrison as they walked over to the cottage. He was taking huge strides that left him feeling like a kid running after a parent.

'What are we looking for?' he asked his back.

'The answer to the question, how the murderer knew when The Horsemen were meeting if he wasn't one of them. It's possible it wasn't through Paul's invites, but as he was the first one killed and the killer was there the night only Paul was invited to the barn, it makes sense that it was Paul's invites being monitored.'

'Yep, I'd concur with that,' Jack replied, knowing full well that it didn't matter whether he agreed or not. He could tell that Harrison had the bit between his teeth on something, and nothing was going to stop him from following its trail.

They came to a screeching halt on the footpath that led up to the front door.

'There's no letter box. No means to post anything through the door,' Harrison said, looking around for some kind of external postbox.

'Could it be a box at the end of the road? That's quite common in more rural areas, avoids the need for the postie to walk up long drives.'

'Could be,' Harrison replied and promptly strode off down the driveway.

Rather than feel like some kind of infant school child trailing after his teacher, Jack headed into the cottage. He'd not looked around it before.

The hallway and sitting-room were a homage to the horse, not surprisingly. On the table there were two plates with fuzzy mould growing across their surface. Neither plate had a fork, just a knife, and Jack guessed those had been bagged by forensics.

He wandered from room to room, looking at

the home of a ghost man, and feeling his own mortality. Here one day. Gone the next.

Somebody would have to come and clear Paul's belongings out one day soon. Perhaps it would be his parents, or maybe Richard would arrange for a stranger to box everything up so that those who had known Paul didn't have to see his life reduced to cardboard containers.

Jack walked over to where some letters sat on the side and peered at the address. *Three Oaks Stables Cottage* it read. That didn't help work out how the letter had got there.

The sound of heavy footsteps crunching up the path and the door being opened let him know Harrison had returned from his hunt.

'Found it?' he asked.

'It's one postbox, at the end of the lane that leads into the yard. We need to find out who has access to it. Someone has to collect the mail each day. Maybe one of the CCTV cameras captured them.'

With that, Harrison disappeared again. Jack sighed, took one last look at Paul Lester's home, and closed the front door. He had to jog to catch-up with Harrison's fast disappearing back.

Harrison took a different route around the staff accommodation block this time, because he was heading to Scott's office, where he guessed the

CCTV cameras might be monitored. It would explain how Scott was always so quick to greet people as they arrived in the yard. As he rounded the old hay loft, he nearly tripped over a pile of old horseshoes, rusting in a mound. He quickened his pace.

Scott's office door was closed. Harrison banged on it and tried the handle. It was locked. He spun around to head back up to the house just as Jack caught up with him.

'Scott's not in,' he said to him as he walked past determinedly.

Richard answered the banging on his door with a weary face.

'We need access to the CCTV camera recordings,' Harrison said bluntly.

'That's Scott's department. Try his office.'

'He's not in, it's locked.'

'Really? OK, he must have popped out for some supplies. Give me a moment and I'll get the spare key for the office door.'

Richard disappeared back into the house, but didn't invite Harrison or Jack in with him.

'I have the feeling he's getting tired of us,' Jack said with a smile.

Harrison didn't smile back.

'What are you thinking?' Jack asked him, recognising that face.

'I'm thinking we're getting close to our man,' Harrison replied, somewhat cryptically.

Jack was about to ask for more information when Richard reappeared with a key. Harrison held out his hand.

'If you don't mind, I'll let you in,' Richard said to him.

Harrison put his hand down and stepped to one side.

The three of them processioned back to the stable office. Past the boxes of thoroughbred horses, most of whom were too busy munching or snoozing, to bother looking at them pass.

'How did Scott get his leg injury?' Harrison asked.

'The limp? That's his back. Flares up every now and then. He had a particularly nasty fall that ended his jockeying career about a decade or so ago. Killed another lad, a friend of his, outright. A big pile-up it was. Two horses had to be euthanised too.'

'I think I remember that,' Jack said. 'Caused a big wave in racing.'

'It did.' Richard nodded. 'But safety improved as a result. Shame it had to be a death and injury that caused it though.'

They'd arrived at the office door.

'I'm sure Scott won't be long,' Richard said as

he plunged the key into the lock. 'He's the one who knows everything about the CCTV.'

Harrison watched as Richard tried to turn the key, but it stayed static, refusing to budge.

'That's strange,' Richard said, pulling the key back out of the lock and looking at the label on it. The label read, *Spare Stable Office*. He put it back into the key hole, but again it refused to turn.

'Give me a few minutes will you? I'll go and double check there's not another one.'

Richard didn't wait for an answer. He was off up to the house.

Jack looked at Harrison with a raised eyebrow.

'I think I understand what you mean now about getting close,' he said.

29

Richard returned with a handful of keys.

'I'm sure that's the right one,' he said to them, more concerned about finding the right key to his stable office than keeping them happy. He plunged a succession of keys into the lock. None of them worked. 'Maybe there's a knack to it,' he said, putting the original key back in and jiggling it around.

'Got any WD40?' Jack asked hopefully.

'Yeah, in the garage. OK, be right back.'

Richard almost ran off. It was clear he was getting agitated now. There were no windows to peer into the office, and Harrison was getting impatient. He wandered off around the yard, staring up at the CCTV cameras. When he saw

Richard returning with the blue and yellow can of lubricant, he rejoined them at the office door.

Richard squirted some of the lubricant into the lock, spraying it all around, until liquid seeped out and dribbled down the door. Then he put the key back in, jiggled it a bit again and tried to turn it. Nothing.

'Shall I try?' Jack asked.

Richard said nothing but stepped back. His mouth drawn; eyes worried.

'I don't get it,' he said. 'We've not had any locks changed and I know that this key used to fit because I occasionally worked from this office, up until about a year ago.'

'Mr Carter, we have reason to be concerned for a man's safety. Do I have your permission to force entry into this office?' Harrison's patience had worn out.

'Are you serious?' Richard looked from one man to the other.

Jack looked at Harrison. He wasn't sure which man's safety Harrison had in mind, but he nodded solemnly at Richard.

'OK, yes, then do it. If Scott's in danger…' Richard trailed off, his face showing the panic that was building up inside of him.

Harrison walked up to the door and leant on it to test its strength. It didn't look particularly solid.

He used his weight to bounce on it a few times and felt the door frame crack and creak beneath his force.

'Do you need a crowbar or something?' Richard asked.

Harrison didn't reply. He stepped back and then rammed his shoulder and upper torso into the wooden door. A splintering crack met him, and with one last shove, the door swung open in his hand. For a moment, all three men stood there.

'I'd better go in first,' Jack said to them.

Jack walked in tentatively. The office was small. Brick walls had been painted cream to make it look less like a dungeon, and there were some filing cabinets and a desk with a computer screen, plus another smaller desk with a screen that was showing the CCTV output. Jack stepped forward and peered behind the desk.

'Clear. There's no one in here.'

'I still don't understand why that key didn't work,' Richard said, as he followed them into the office.

'How many cameras do you have?' Harrison moved the conversation on.

'Ten, placed around the yard.'

'I only counted nine,' Harrison replied, peering at the screen with the various shots.

'Is there one that covers the end of the drive?'

'Not really the end. There's one that covers the drive itself, so you can see everything coming and going.'

'What kind of car does Scott drive?' he asked Richard.

'An old black Ford Fiesta.'

Harrison clicked on the screen and went into replay mode on the camera that covered the drive. It wasn't long before they saw Scott's car driving out.

'He left fifteen minutes ago. Straight after he'd given us the key for Paul's cottage,' he said to them.

'There's nine camera feeds up. Are you sure there is a tenth?'

'Yeah, positive. Let me take a look.'

Richard took over the mouse and clicked into settings. Sure enough, there was a tenth camera listed, but for some reason it hadn't been added to the monitoring screen. When he ticked the box to add it, a view of Paul's cottage came up.

'Oh, now I never knew we had one looking out over the cottage.' Richard looked panicky. 'I'd have told you when you first came if I knew.'

There were a few moments silence in the office as minds worked feverishly through the mounting evidence. Richard's face had visibly paled by the time Harrison spoke again.

'Who is it that collects the post in the morning?'

'It's Scott.'

'Always?'

'Yes.'

'Mr Carter, we are going to need to take a look in Scott's room.'

'Right. Yes. OK.' Was all he could muster.

Harrison's mobile phone started to vibrate in his pocket, but he ignored it. He was convinced Scott was the killer. That very first day he'd seen him adjust the horse box lock, he should have known he was OCD. It had to be somebody who had access to Paul's post for him to know when The Horsemen invitations arrived. He would have followed him, like Gavin had done, and he could have watched him, monitoring his comings and goings on the CCTV. The big questions was, why?

Richard led them to the old hay barn that now served as staff accommodation. Jack had a quick look around. Inside on the ground floor was a kitchen, relatively new and clean, with stickers on cupboard doors carrying names of people the contents belonged to.

In the middle was a bathroom with shower, bath, and toilet.

'We're ripping out the bathroom next week,' Richard said by way of apology for the tired state of the fittings. Harrison wasn't interested in decor.

At the other end of the ground floor was the sitting-room. They had a quick look in there, but it gave up nothing other than to show it as a place where people relaxed and watched TV. Copies of horse magazines and the Racing Post were scattered around the place, and the fireplace looked like some work had recently been done to it, with a new heater in situ.

'That's where they found the cat.' Richard pointed at the chimney area.

Upstairs, there was a narrow corridor with four doors. Two along the front wall, two along the back. There was the sound of music playing.

'This is Scott's room,' Richard said, arriving at the second door along the back, opposite the one where they could hear music. 'I feel like we're invading his privacy doing this.'

'We can take it from here,' Jack said. He took the key from Richard's hand and put on a pair of gloves. At the sight of them, Richard stepped back.

'Please stay here, Mr Carter,' Jack said to him.

Jack opened the door and stepped in first. Harrison knew to hang back, but without even entering the room, he could see the row of horseshoes which had been nailed above the door frame.

What met Jack's eyes was an incredibly neat and tidy room, one where it was clear that everything had its place. The bed was immaculately made up, even the curtains seemed to have been straightened in neat, equal pleats. The next thing that struck him was the big crucifix above the bed.

'No one here. What should we be looking for?' Jack called back to Harrison.

'OK for me to come in?'

'Sure, put some gloves on.' Jack handed Harrison a pair of gloves from his pocket.

'Do you mind giving me some space?'

'Course,' Jack replied, and stepped back into the corridor with Richard.

Harrison stood for a moment, grounding himself in the room. His eyes covered every inch, taking in the detail, logging and categorising all he saw. The room was so clean and tidy it could only belong to someone with some kind of obsessive-compulsive disorder. No one else would feel the need to have regimentally lined up every item on the top of the chest of drawers in order of size, as Scott had. He opened a drawer and saw colour coded socks all neatly wrapped together like some kind of weird painting palette.

The huge crucifix above the bed, was joined by horseshoes which were fixed to every single wall, and particularly clustered above the window and door. Harrison was convinced he'd found their killer. All he needed was one final piece of proof, and they could arrest him with confidence.

Harrison's mobile rang again in his pocket. He wished he'd turned it off, it was distracting.

He blocked it out. He had to put himself into the mind of Scott. Where would he hide two human hearts which he believed were going to protect him from the evil spirits of their original hosts? They had to be in this room. This was his sanctuary. It would be while he slept that he'd fear the most.

Harrison went straight for the bed. In keeping with the rest of the tidiness, he'd not expected to see anything underneath it. What he found were two shoeboxes, one at the head end, one at the bottom end. He carefully pulled one from under the bed, touching it as little as possible. Tentatively he took the lid off, not sure what sight or smell he might find. Inside was a wooden box. It had held some kind of horse medical supplies. Harrison lifted it out, breathing a sigh of relief when he saw it wasn't lockable.

Carefully, he eased the lid open with a

fingertip, and once he'd seen what he'd been expecting to see, he flipped it open.

'Jack, get onto control and put out an order for the arrest of Scott Smith.'

Jack stepped back into the room.

'What the hell is that?'

'It's what they call a witch's bottle. You use it to ward off evil spells and spirits from someone you believe could be cursing you or using magic against you.'

'Is that?' Jack asked, pointing at the contents.

'Yep, it's a human heart pierced with an iron nail, and probably in human urine. The other objects might be horse hoof shavings. There's a second box underneath the bed.'

'Eugh,' was all Jack could reply.

'What's going on? Why do you want to arrest Scott?' Richard started to come into the room.

'Mr Carter, I'm going to have to ask you to leave please. This is now a crime scene.' Jack sprang back to the door and ushered the shocked Richard back out.

'Jack?' Harrison said, thinking. 'We need to find out where Scott's gone.'

'You think he could be after another one?'

'If he's worried that we're getting close then perhaps he's throwing caution to the wind.'

'Mr Carter, I need to know Scott's mobile

number please, and his car registration,' Jack said, dialling the incident room as he spoke and thrusting a notebook and pen under Richard's nose for the details. 'I need a trace on a car and mobile phone,' he said into his phone, walking away from Richard so he could talk more freely.

While Jack was talking to control, Harrison stood in Scott's room with one unanswered question. Why was it that Scott latched on to Paul Lester? Why had he seen The Horsemen as a threat? Was it simply that he was jealous of Paul's success?

He turned to the wardrobe. He didn't want to touch too much, as forensics would want to go over the room, but there had to be an answer somewhere.

When he opened the wardrobe door, he was met by the same immaculate neatness as the rest of the room. On a top shelf were some jumpers neatly folded, and alongside these was a cardboard box. Harrison couldn't resist. He took the box down and placed it on the floor, crouching down to open the lid and look at its contents.

Inside was a selection of newspaper cuttings, dating back over a decade. They started with stories of Scott's success as a jockey, but by far the majority of them related to the accident which had ended his racing career.

'Pile-up kills jockey and horses' was one headline, 'Racing mourns after fatal fall' was another. There was a photograph of a young jockey, Cliff Cunningham, who had broken his neck and died instantly following a four-horse pile-up at a jump.

Harrison skimmed through the cutting. Scott Smith was mentioned as having to be stretchered off with a back injury in the pile-up, while another jockey broke his leg and pelvis. Then right at the bottom it was mentioned that novice jockey, Paul Lester, miraculously avoided injury, walking away from the scene unharmed. That was it. It all made sense. Paul had escaped without a scratch, while Scott was seriously injured and his friend killed. Scott must have been in hospital for months following the accident, but while they mended his back, they'd probably not attended to the post-traumatic stress disorder the accident had caused. Harrison could bet he'd mended physically, but not received any treatment for the mental scars. It would have been the start of an obsession as to why Paul had managed to avoid injury when the others hadn't.

Harrison put the cuttings back into the wardrobe and rejoined Richard Carter in the corridor. The man was not looking too well.

'This could ruin me. I built these stables up

from nothing. My reputation is everything,' he said to Harrison when he reappeared.

'Are you saying you're involved?' Harrison asked him.

'No! Of course not,' Richard replied angrily.

'Then your reputation will remain intact,' Harrison simply replied.

'I don't think you understand…' Richard began.

'Mr Carter, do you know who or what caused the accident that injured Scott?'

Richard looked at Harrison, surprised by the sudden question at such a time.

'Yes, there was a huge enquiry, but it was pretty obvious. It was a loose horse, she'd lost her jockey and they'd not managed to catch her. They should have stopped the race, but they didn't, and she ran across them just as they all landed after a jump. There was nothing any of the jockeys could have done because they couldn't see she was there. The front pack were well ahead of the rest of the field luckily and they were flagged down, otherwise it would have been even worse. Horse racing is a very dangerous sport, Dr Lane. You have powerful beasts with minds of their own, travelling at up to forty miles per hour with men balanced on top of them.'

'Yes, I think I'm learning just how dangerous it is,' Harrison replied.

Just then the door from which music could be heard was opened and the sound of electro-pop filled the corridor.

'All right, Richard?' the head which appeared around the door asked.

'Yeah, all fine, Todd,' he replied.

Todd eyeballed Harrison.

'Don't suppose you know where Scott went do you?' Harrison asked him.

The head shook.

'No. Saw him about half an hour ago rooting around in that pile of old horseshoes but didn't speak to him. He's probably gone to hammer a few more shoes around the place, you know what he's like with them.'

Harrison did know what he was like with them, and it wasn't using them for luck that he was worried about.

'Mr Carter, I need you to seal this room and not allow anyone in until other officers arrive. Is that clear? If anyone enters this room after we've gone, they will be charged with perverting the course of justice. There are officers on their way.'

'I understand,' Richard replied. 'So, what are you suggesting? That Scott killed Paul? Is that what you're saying? I can't believe it, that's crazy.'

He pulled Scott's door closed and locked it.

'If Scott returns, you must call 999 immediately. We have reason to believe that he's dangerous.'

'My God, he spends time alone with my children.' Richard had turned ashen white.

'He has a clear motive in his mind, and probably believed he was helping protect you and your family too,' Harrison said to him as his parting words. He had to find Jack fast before they had another victim.

Jack was outside pacing up and down on the phone.

'Jack, we need to go,' he said to him. 'He's not gone shopping, he's gone after his next victim.'

'How do you know?' Jack asked.

'He's picked up some more iron horseshoes.'

'But who? There are about a dozen possibles, how are we going to know which one he's targeting.'

'My guess is he's going to go for the one closest to Paul, Craig Matlock, and he's got a long head start so we'd better hurry.'

30

Tanya cancelled the call she was making on her mobile. It had gone through to Harrison's voicemail for a second time. He was obviously busy. She was going to have to deal with this situation on her own.

DCI Barker had called her about ten minutes ago to tell her that the Scottish sociopath had not turned up for the interview about his murdered girlfriend. She sounded concerned about what he was up to.

'Are you safe where you are?' she'd asked her. 'I need you to be on your guard in case he's decided that we're on to him and he throws caution to the wind.'

'I'm fine,' Tanya had replied, but she should have been honest. She'd forgotten a few things that she needed from her flat and had decided to go and pick them up while she thought her stalker would be otherwise occupied in a police interview. Only now it turned out that he wasn't there at all.

'Tanya, promise me that if you're worried, you'll call 999 immediately? It's on the system now so it will be treated as a priority emergency. Any issues, you have my number.'

'Thank you, yes. I will and I'll be fine.'

The second she'd ended the call with the DCI, she nearly slapped herself for being so stupid. Why wasn't she honest with her? Or why didn't she just turn right around and go back to her friend's flat right now? The problem was, she'd already reached the end of her road. If he was here, he'd have already seen her. She'd gone past the point of no return and if he was waiting he'd just follow her there and she'd potentially put her friend in danger too.

Tanya hadn't wanted to worry Harrison, but she had wanted his advice. Would the stalker be likely to come after her, or is he long gone on a boat out of the country? Would he attack even though it might be dangerous for him? Whatever the answers he might have given, she was about to find out for herself.

It's really difficult to walk when you think somebody might be watching you. You become aware of every little movement you make. The act of placing one foot in front of the other, something that's so automatic and easy to most people, suddenly involves a great deal of conscious thought. Was he here? Was he watching her now?

Every molecule in her body seemed to be on high alert. She wondered if this is what it felt like to be a rabbit grazing on open ground, aware that danger could come from anywhere. Left. Right. Behind. Above.

Her breathing was shallow, and she could already feel a pain in her neck from where she held her shoulders so stiffly. She wanted to keep looking around her, but it would be so obvious. Did that matter? Would he be less likely to attack her if he knew she was aware?

Tanya reached the house. She looked around. There was nobody. She was being paranoid.

Down the steps. She had her key ready in her pocket in case she'd needed to get in quick. The one downside with adding an extra lock to the front door was that it now took twice as long to get in.

The key went into the first lock and it clicked to open, just one more to go.

She put the key into the second lock. Click, and the door was open.

She felt him almost before she heard him.

It was like a whoosh as he jumped from the stairs above and landed behind her. The black crow swooping down.

There wasn't even time to cry out. No time to turn to face him. He shoved her in the back and sent her sprawling onto the floor of her hallway, crashing down onto her knees and elbows. The crow had attacked.

31

Harrison drove while Jack spent the entire journey on the phone with Cambridgeshire police control or the incident room. The first priority was to make sure all the rest of The Horsemen were safe. Jack arranged for them to be called and then have a uniformed officer go out to every one of them. It was a huge draw on resources, but both men knew that at least one of them was in danger. As they drove, the reports came back that there were two that couldn't be accounted for. They weren't answering their phones. One of them was Craig Matlock.

When Jack finally came off the phone, Harrison filled him in on what he'd found in the wardrobe, and his conversation with Richard.

'So he's harboured a grudge against Paul all these years.'

'In his mind it's not a grudge. He's tried to rationalise why Paul walked away from that accident without a scratch, when his best friend, who was a more experienced jockey, died. But of course, he couldn't rationalise it, so he turned it into a belief that Paul is protected by a greater force. When he saw the fake hanging in the barn, it would have tipped him over the edge. He'd have been convinced Paul was involved in some kind of black magic which meant he couldn't die.'

'And Sam?' Jack asked.

'He would have thought Paul was recruiting more like him.'

'I hope we're not too late, he'll have been at Craig's farm for up to twenty minutes already.'

It was a tense eight-minute ride through narrow country lanes to Craig Matlock's farm. Both of them knew that a man's life depended on someone getting there fast. When they arrived in the yard, there was no sign of any patrol cars yet, but there was a black Ford Fiesta.

'Craig?' Jack jumped straight out of the car and ran over to the house, shouting out to him and hammering on the door and windows. Harrison headed into the barn where they'd seen him take his horse. He ran into the dark interior, mindful that Scott could be in there with a weapon. His eyes struggled to adjust to the darkness. In front, he could see a horse blanket flopped over the door of a stall. Harrison headed straight for it. The gelding they'd seen Craig grooming at their last visit, looked up startled at his sudden appearance. There was no sign of Craig.

He checked in all the other stalls, trying to adjust his eyes to the darkness. There was nobody. He listened. Nothing but the horse.

By the time Harrison returned to the yard, Jack had finished his check around the house and was just appearing from round the side.

'I can't see anything in the house, not unless he's holding him in there. We'd have to break down the door,' he said to Harrison.

'Can I help you?' a loud, rather accusatory voice asked from behind them.

Harrison turned to see a man walking towards them from the huge new barn, which was filled with agricultural equipment.

'We're looking for Craig,' Jack explained.

'He's in demand today. Just told another fella where to find him. They went to the old barn.'

'Thanks,' Jack shouted as he burst into a run behind the already disappearing back of Harrison Lane.

Harrison ran at full pelt down the narrow lane which led to the old barn. The ground was uneven, and he nearly twisted his ankle a few times, weaving around, trying to avoid the dips and bumps.

In his head, he was working out how Scott was going to try to overpower Craig. Would he try to hang him again like Paul, or simply stab him and get it over and done with. Harrison hoped it was the former because that would take longer. They might not be too late.

Behind him, Harrison could hear the pounding feet and panting breath of Jack, and in the distance a police siren that seemed to be getting closer. That was all he was aware of, because his total focus was getting to the wooden structure which had come into view in front of him, in time to save Craig Matlock.

The barn door was ajar, and Harrison burst through it, coming to a screeching halt. There was nobody there. The ground floor was empty.

Then he looked up and saw them. Scott was in the hayloft, and at his feet was a slumped figure. He was putting the noose around his neck.

'Scott,' he shouted, trying desperately to make his voice sound as calm and even as he could. He was puffed after the run, so it wasn't easy and the stress had made his voice rise an octave. 'It's Dr

Lane. Please stop what you're doing and come down and talk to me.' He paused to catch his breath and breathe. 'I understand why you're doing this, but you need to know that the hangings you witnessed were fake. The Horsemen ritual was fake. Those men fell into a pile of hay, they were not hung.'

Scott had momentarily stopped what he was doing and stared at Harrison.

'You're lying,' he said. 'I saw it with my own eyes. They swore their souls to Satan, and he brought them back.'

'No. You only saw half of it. They untied the rope and the men just fell unharmed. Please, Scott, we need to talk this through. Richard is worried. He needs you back at the yard. He needs your help.'

Scott hesitated. He was staring at Harrison. For a moment, he seemed to go into a trance.

From the corner of his eye, Harrison could see that Jack had also come into the barn, but less obtrusively. He'd crept around the right edge until he reached the ladder to the hayloft and started to climb.

Harrison tried to keep Scott's attention and walked forward so that he was standing in front of Scott but below him, where the pile of hay once sat. If Scott focused on him, that gave Jack the best chance of creeping up behind him unnoticed.

'The yard can't run without you being there, Scott. Leave Craig and we can head back and talk to Richard.'

Harrison could see the tug of war between his loyalty to Richard and the obsession with killing The Horsemen.

Scott wavered. Then the movement of Jack crowning the top of the ladder made him turn. He tightened the noose around Craig's neck and got ready to shove him over the ledge. Jack rushed at him in a desperate attempt to reach him before he could push Craig over.

As Jack grabbed his arms, Scott kicked out with one final shove at Craig. Pushing his unconscious body over the edge.

There was a loud thump as both Jack and Scott hit the deck of the wooden hay loft platform. Jack on top.

'Scott Smith, I'm arresting you for the suspected murders of Paul Lester and Sam Brown.' He wrestled some handcuffs onto the squirming Scott. 'You do not have to say anything, but it may harm your defence if you do not mention when questioned something which you later rely on in court. Anything you do say may be given in evidence.'

Grateful that he was the larger man, Jack pulled Scott into a position where he could handcuff him to the ring that held the other end of the hanging rope. As soon as Scott was secure, Jack took a few deep breaths and turned to look over the edge with dread. He expected to see Craig Matlock swinging mid-air, neck broken or his face gradually reddening as the rope crushed his airways.

Instead, he saw the tall, muscular frame of Harrison Lane, straining to hold Craig's unconscious body so that the rope remained limp, and the noose stayed loose around his neck.

Harrison looked up at Jack, his face red with the exertion.

'A hand down here would be good,' he said. 'In your own time.'

32

Harrison and Jack released the noose from Craig's neck and got him to the ground in safety. He still had a relatively strong pulse, but a gash on the back of his head suggested Scott had knocked him unconscious.

Before Jack even had the chance to call it in, the patrol car arrived outside, and the officers were quickly on their radios for paramedic support.

Both Jack and Harrison were grateful to be able to sit down while the ambulance crew attended to Craig. The huge rush of adrenaline, combined with the physical effort, had drained them.

They watched as the paramedics worked on Craig.

'His vital signs are strong,' one of them said. 'He'll be fine.'

'Are *you* OK?' Jack asked Harrison.

He'd been rubbing his arms and rolling his shoulders.

'I'm fine. It was a bit of a jolt catching Craig, but I'm OK, no real damage done. Luckily it wasn't a big drop.'

The uniformed officers retrieved Scott down from the hayloft and took him into custody.

'That will be an insanity plea,' Jack muttered after he'd walked out.

'Probably. He needs proper treatment. I think he has some kind of post-traumatic stress disorder after the accident. They got him walking again, but they didn't deal with the mental injuries.'

'You do realise that Scott's now going to be even more convinced that The Horsemen are immortal,' said Jack. 'As far as he was concerned, he pushed Craig off that edge to his death.'

'I don't think Craig will need to worry about Scott anymore.'

'Any sign of O'Neil?' Jack asked.

'Not yet.'

'I can tell by your voice that you're looking forward to seeing the expression on his face, as much as I am, when he realises we've solved his case for him,' Jack smirked.

Harrison raised an eyebrow and gave a wry smile back.

'It's been a successful week all round for me.' Jack smiled, thinking about Marie.

'Indeed, but I need to head back to London in the morning. I've done what I came to do,' Harrison said to Jack.

'I'll stay here until the end of the week. It's doing Marie the world of good, and I'll need to deal with all the paperwork anyway.'

Harrison's mind had wandered back to thoughts of Tanya. It reminded him that he hadn't checked his phone in a while. Hadn't there been someone trying to ring him earlier? He pulled his phone from his pocket. Two missed calls came up. Both were from Tanya.

He dialled back immediately.

There was no reply.

He dialled again.

'Everything OK?' Jack asked. Harrison's face had lost the earlier relief and humour. He looked worried.

'I missed a couple of calls from Tanya,' Harrison replied. 'Now she's not answering.'

'She's probably in a meeting or at a job,' Jack reassured him.

'I promised to be available,' Harrison replied.

He searched for DCI Barker's number and dialled.

'Harrison, I was about to call you,' DCI Barker answered her phone. She sounded a little breathy. In Harrison's experience, that was rarely a good thing. It indicated heightened stress levels.

'Tanya's stalker failed to turn up for his appointment and now we aren't having any luck in contacting her. I spoke to her earlier and she said she was fine, but she didn't go back to her friend's house. Has she called you?'

Harrison's heart froze. She'd called him twice. She was in trouble.

'She called earlier. I couldn't answer.'

'Don't worry. I'm sure she's fine we're dealing with it. We'll find her.'

HARRISON HAD NEVER CHECKED out of a hotel so fast. Jack had instructed one of the uniformed officers to drive him back to the station on blue lights. Once there, he'd got straight on his bike. He had no remorse running off like this. He'd done what he'd promised to do. The rest was police work. Jack could take care of the interviews, he understood the case. He needed to be in London, where he should have been when Tanya had needed him.

The ride down to London was hell. He couldn't look at his phone, so he had no idea if anyone was trying to call him again, and he couldn't try to ring Tanya to see if she was OK. All the way, a thousand different scenarios were going through his mind. The cold, dead eyes of the Scottish sociopath filled his head and each time they were looking at a terrified Tanya, helpless, immobilised. About to meet her death.

The grip of fear and guilt for not being there froze his heart and clawed at his insides. This was exactly the reason why he avoided relationships. The pain and sense of responsibility was overwhelming.

The minute he arrived on the outskirts of London and was able to pull over, he checked his phone. Nothing. He called Tanya's mobile. No reply. He rang DCI Barker. No reply.

He couldn't waste any more time, he had to carry on.

The London traffic was more frustrating than ever. Every selfish driver seemed to be out on the roads, determined not to let motorbikes through. He nearly scratched the side of one car, but he didn't care. The driver shouted at him through the window. A string of expletives in a heavy foreign accent. He rode on regardless.

Tanya could be petrified, being held captive.

Injured, or worse still. If anything had happened to her, he would never forgive himself.

Why hadn't he answered his phone earlier. He'd told her to call if she needed him. He'd promised to be there for her.

Where would he have taken her? Should he go to her friend's flat? That's where she should be. No, DCI Barker said they'd tried there. Maybe her flat? She could be anywhere in London. He might have snatched her from the streets or lured her to a location somewhere that nobody could hear her scream.

He didn't know enough about the man yet, but the most obvious place was going to be her flat. There, he could terrify her in her own place of safety. The place he'd been watching and probably fantasising about getting inside. Would DCI Barker have sent someone to her flat already? Or was Tanya locked in there with him, too scared to call out, or gagged and bound, awaiting death?

Harrison made a decision. He would start at the beginning of the trail. He would go to her flat. He would find her. He had to.

Every yard on his bike seemed to take forever. He wished each road to pass by quicker. Prayed for the traffic lights to stay green. Risked death by pulling out in front of buses and lorries.

Harrison was just minutes away. He could see her flat in his mind's eye. He willed himself to get there faster.

Finally, he started to recognise the neighbourhood. There was the café he'd hidden in after seeing the sociopath for the first time.

Harrison turned into her road.

He saw them immediately. You couldn't miss them. Two police patrol cars, lights still flashing, and an ambulance in the middle of the road. Right outside Tanya's flat.

Harrison screeched to a halt and jumped off his bike. Running the last few yards to her front door.

Two police officers were standing in the open doorway. Had they had to break-in?

He vaulted down the steps.

'Is she OK? Where's Tanya?' he asked the first police officer who turned to see who he was. Harrison peered around him. Inside, he could see the hallway table tipped over on the floor.

'I'm sorry sir, you can't come in here.' The officer held his hand up and went to block Harrison.

He pulled out his police ID and shouted, 'Tanya?'

The officer looked at the ID as Harrison went to step into the flat. He stopped as two other officers came towards the door from the sitting-room. Between them was the Scottish sociopath in handcuffs. They had him. But where was Tanya?

'We've arrested him, Dr Lane,' the officer said to him. 'It's a crime scene, I can't let you in right now.' The young officer tried to reassure him.

Harrison stepped aside as the two officers led the stalker from Tanya's flat. He walked out; head held high. There was blood on his face. It looked like his nose might be broken because it was now at a different angle to what it had been before, and Harrison could see the swelling starting. Despite this and the pain he must have been in, there was no emotion on his face. He looked at Harrison. His eyes narrowed slightly, and he saw the glimmer of recognition cross the man's face. Then he was gone.

Harrison couldn't stand it any longer. No matter what he was going to find in there, he had to see her. He dived straight into the flat before the other officers could say a word to stop him.

'Tanya,' he shouted into the flat.

'Please, Dr Lane, this is a crime scene.' He heard the officer behind him say.

Then he saw her. In the sitting-room on the sofa. The sight took his breath away, stopping him so fast that he had to put a hand out to prevent himself from losing his balance.

She looked so beautiful. Pale, but beautiful.

She didn't seem to have been touched. There wasn't a mark on her.

'Harrison.' Tanya's face lit up when she saw his. She jumped up from the sofa and reached out for him.

For a few moments he couldn't speak.

'Are you all right? I've been so worried,' he said, enveloping her in his arms, folding her into his chest.

'Yes, I'm fine.'

'I thought he'd…' Harrison couldn't even finish the words.

'I told you,' she said, looking up at him. 'He was messing with the wrong woman. He jumped me when I came home, took me by surprise and pushed me into the flat just as I'd unlocked the door. But I'd prepared. I had weapons everywhere. I got him first with hairspray in his eyes. I pressed the panic alarm as he tried to get over that, and when he came after me, I used the baseball bat. He'd expected me to be too scared to fight back, but he was wrong. I wasn't going to be his next victim.'

'You clever girl. I should have known you'd outsmart him.'

Harrison breathed in deeply, pulling the scent of her into his mind and body. As he let the breath go, he felt the last hour's tension release from him, and his shoulders drop by at least two inches.

'I'm glad you're here now, though,' Tanya whispered.

Harrison looked into her eyes and allowed himself to be pulled straight down into their depths. He released her from his arms and gently took her face in his hands. Her skin was so soft and smooth. His thumb caressed her cheek and he bent forward, allowing his lips to meet hers. They were as sweet and soft as he'd imagined they would be.

33

Two weeks later, Harrison and Jack were in a conference room wrapping up a telephone call with DCI Robert Whittaker. He had everything sewn up. Scott was being given a full psychological assessment and was currently detained in a secure unit. Craig had fully recovered and confirmed he was officially disbanding The Horsemen. He was talking to his father about letting the barn be used by the Wildlife Trust as a visitor centre and educational area. The Cambridgeshire team was preparing everything for a trial and DCI Whittaker was yet again thanking the pair of them for their assistance.

As soon as they'd ended the call, Jack spun round to Harrison.

'I've found something, well someone, who knows about the Nunhead murder.'

Harrison was taken aback. Jack had promised to help him find his mother's killer, but he'd no idea that he'd already made some progress.

'I was able to use her DNA sample and matched it to living relatives. Her parents are gone, but she still has a sister who's alive, and she lives in London. I've already phoned her, and she's confirmed that her sister went missing in 1993 and hasn't been heard of since. She's more than willing to talk to us.'

Harrison didn't know what to say.

'You OK?' Jack asked, concern replacing his usual cheeky face.

'Thank you. Definitely.'

'OK, I'll sort out a time and let you know. She works in the day so it will probably have to be either an evening or weekend.'

'Whatever, that's fine.'

'Sure you won't be too busy with Dr Jones?' Jack teased.

Harrison hadn't lived down the moment that DCI Barker walked into Tanya's flat to find the pair of them kissing. He'd been mortified by the interruption, first because he'd been enjoying the moment so much, and second because the news spread around the station faster than a dose of

Norovirus, and Jack had been mercilessly teasing him about it ever since. Fake *Love Island* posters with his and Tanya's photos on had been stuck around his office and the incident room. It had all been a bit overwhelming, especially when Ryan had to explain to him what *Love Island* was. Harrison had a very strong suspicion as to who was behind the posters too, and he wasn't sitting too far away from him.

Harrison was nervous about meeting the sister of the Nunhead murder victim. It was a very dark period of his life, a horror that he and his mother had run away from and the truth of which lay buried deep inside his mind. Although it was a long time ago, and he'd been a child, he still felt some kind of responsibility for having been there that night. It was his hunt for answers, though that drove him on. He would never get justice for his mother, or the Nunhead victim, unless he faced up to his own fears.

Her sister was very keen to see them, desperate that they might finally have some news. The family had been searching all this time, hoping that one day they too would get some answers. The next evening, Jack and Harrison drove up to a small terraced house in North London.

Harrison had no idea where this might lead him in his hunt for justice, but every step he took towards proving that Desmond and Freda Manning were killers was a step in the right direction.

The woman who opened the door took him by surprise initially. She was in her fifties and finding keeping the weight off hard. Dressed in practical jeans and a baggy top, Elizabeth Ward looked nothing like the ethereal dark-haired beauty that had lain in a white dress on the stone in Nunhead Cemetery. Harrison had kept her sister locked inside his head for so long that he'd forgotten she would have aged had she been allowed to live.

Elizabeth was a social worker, specialising in problem teenagers. It was clear her work meant a lot to her. In the sitting-room, she proudly displayed the awards and certificates she'd received throughout her career. Also on the wall was a photograph of Elizabeth as a young woman. Her grey streaked hair had once been dark, just like he remembered the girl in Nunhead.

Jack had a photograph of the Jane Doe they now believed to be Annette Ward. A young woman who would have been just twenty-two at the time of her death. He didn't need to get it out to show Elizabeth to know that they'd finally confirmed her identity. Elizabeth had several photographs already spread out across the table in the sitting-room. They were of two young attractive women, in the prime of their lives, dressed up to go out, or laughing at a party. There was also one of Annette, looking pensive and withdrawn, a sadness in her face.

'I'm very sorry,' Jack started, 'I believe that it's quite likely that the young woman who died in 1993 is indeed your sister, Annette.'

Tears instantly welled in Elizabeth's eyes.

'I knew she was dead. She had to be. There was no way she'd not have got in contact with us.'

'We will need some formal identification procedures, but I'm fairly confident that with the DNA trace and the photographs we have, it is your sister.'

'What happened to her?' Elizabeth asked now, her voice wavering.

'She was stabbed and killed in Nunhead Cemetery.'

'Nunhead? The last we'd heard she was in Wales,' Elizabeth said.

At the mention of Wales, Harrison's heart was clutched by an icy fist. Flashes from his childhood lit up his mind. He wanted to get up from the comfortable leather sofa in Elizabeth Ward's house and run. Run away into the dark streets outside, where he didn't have to face the ghosts that haunted his mind.

'Have they have caught her killer?' Elizabeth's broken voice brought him back to reality. He had to focus. There were other victims, not just him.

Jack shook his head. 'I'm afraid not yet, but that's one of the reasons why we're here talking to you now. We wanted to know as much about Annette's life and who she might have been spending time with.'

'She'd been fine, you know, just got a bit lost in her late teens and made some bad choices. I think her first boyfriend was what you'd call a gaslighter nowadays. He was very manipulative, wrecked her confidence and made her withdraw into herself. Eventually he dumped her, but the damage was done and she ended up seeking spiritual help to find herself.'

'What about your parents?'

'That was part of the issue. My parents were overseas in Hong Kong with Dad's work. My sister and I had decided we wanted to go back to the UK. I was twenty-three, and she was twenty-one, old enough to look after ourselves and make up our own minds where we wanted to live. Then I got a job offer in Edinburgh and left Annette here. I wasn't doing social work then. I was training to be a legal secretary. It was only after Annette disappeared I changed careers. Wanted to help other young people like her. Guilt, I suppose. I've always felt like I abandoned her. Maybe this wouldn't have happened if I'd been around.'

'You can't know that, Ms Ward. Everyone makes their own choices. Were you not aware of the publicity following her murder? Investigators tried to find next of kin, but nobody came forward.'

'I wasn't. As far as I knew, Annette had taken up with some kind of cult in Wales. I didn't hear from her from one month to the next. I was enjoying life in Edinburgh. I didn't have any friends in London.'

'Do you know who she was with in Wales?' Harrison found his voice. Now he was desperate to know everything.

'Yeah, we told the police when we reported her missing about six months later. It wasn't far from the Brecon Beacons. I've got a note of it somewhere. But when I went down there, they just denied she'd ever been there. They wouldn't let me in and every single one of them denied having ever seen her. It was my word against all theirs.'

Harrison's stomach twisted as he listened to Elizabeth.

'Llanfynydd,' he almost whispered.

'Yes. Yes, that's it,' Elizabeth replied. She flicked through some paperwork she had on the table.

'Yes, just outside of Llanfynydd village. They were quite remote. The two people who ran it were called Desmond and Freda Manning. It was supposed to be a spiritual awakening centre, that's how they advertised it, but I had serious doubts about what they did. It was like some kind of brain washing cult to me. I'd seen Annette just the once after she'd joined, and she was even more withdrawn than before. She almost seemed scared. I asked her if she was OK, promised my help if she needed it, but she would just say no. I can still see her, the way she looked the last time. She was pale and thin, dressed in a faded brown jumpsuit. Her hair looked like it hadn't been brushed in days and she kept fiddling with the necklace she always wore.'

'It was a crystal, a purple crystal. An amethyst?' Harrison suddenly said. He had no idea where that had come from, but it was there, the image of her in his head. He saw her smiling and laughing with him, the crystal catching the light. She'd been trapped inside his mind all those years.

'Yes, it was. Was it still with her?'

'No, they didn't find it with her body, I'm afraid,' Jack replied, throwing a concerned look at Harrison.

'Then how do you…?'

'My mother was there too, in Wales,' said Harrison. 'I was there. I was only five or six, but when you described her, I remembered Annette.'

'My God. Then do you know what happened to her?'

Harrison shook his head and looked away from her. The shame was back, the feeling of guilt that he hadn't helped Annette or his mother. The feeling that there was more in his mind he should remember, but it was out of his reach.

He didn't say another word until it was time to say goodbye. Jack carried the whole conversation and promised Elizabeth that they would be back in touch to make a formal identification and look to see if the case could be officially re-opened.

Harrison said goodbye to Elizabeth and took his secret away with him. She'd had enough shock for one day. He wasn't going to tell her what he believed in his heart; that her sister had been killed as a sacrifice to Satan.

34

The meeting with Elizabeth knocked Harrison sideways. For years he'd known there were hidden memories, images which haunted him, buried deep in his mind where he couldn't access them. As the years had gone on, he'd started to think maybe he had imagined things, that his childish fantasy had taken over and twisted what he'd seen. Over in America, the misty pictures in his mind's eye had drifted further and further away. Talking to Elizabeth seemed to have opened a bridge to those memories.

Now he had proof that there were others who were there. Others who had seen what he'd seen, and he knew his instincts hadn't been wrong. His mother had been murdered by the Mannings.

. . .

Since Tanya's ordeal with her stalker, Harrison had only seen her a few times. A lot of the problem had been work; their diary commitments clashed, but if he was honest, he'd been making excuses. The power of his feelings for her had taken him by surprise. He knew that when he was in her presence, he struggled to resist. So he avoided her.

One thing about Tanya that Harrison was learning was that she wasn't a woman who gave up easily. He was sitting at his desk, deep in thought about the meaning behind a passage of text found at a church break-in, when a text came through from her.

Hi stranger, wondered if it would be possible for you to come round after work. Need a hand with something. Will pay with dinner.

Harrison's heart jumped and his stomach flipped. Why did his body betray him every time he saw anything to do with her? What did she need him for? He looked up at Ryan, as though he may have somehow noticed his change in demeanour. He was focused on his screen as usual.

Sure. 6.30pm OK?

Perfect. See you then

Now his stomach began a dance of anticipation. He looked at his watch; he had seven hours to get through.

Harrison had gone home for a shower and for a change of clothes. It wasn't that he felt particularly grubby, but it filled the time and kept his mind off his impending arrival at Tanya's flat. As it was, he arrived outside at twenty-five past six and took several deep breaths before heading down the steps and knocking.

When Tanya opened her front door, it was obvious that she too had come home, showered, and changed after work. She had her hair down in waves over her shoulders and a cream and pink dress on that enhanced her eyes and hair colour.

'Harrison, thanks so much for coming round.' She ushered him in with a kiss on his cheek. 'How's your week been?' she continued cheerfully.

'Fine. Yours?' he asked.

'Yeah, good, actually. Nothing too gruesome this week, so that's always a bonus, and I had a day out on a course earlier this week. Tiring but useful and nice to do something different.'

'You said you needed my help?'

'Ah yes.' She smiled, and he followed as she led him out to her patio. 'I hope you don't mind, but I really wanted that plant pot moving from here over to there. Sorry to have to ask you, but there's just no way I can budge it.'

'Of course,' Harrison said, and within thirty seconds had shifted the blue glazed pot across her tiny patio. It hadn't actually felt that heavy at all. 'What else?' He looked around for the rest of what she needed doing.

'That's it.'

He turned to look at her, puzzled. She was beaming at him, watching his face.

'Sorry. It was an excuse to get you round for dinner. I was worried you were avoiding me.'

'No. I'm not.'

'Are you sure? Do you regret what happened? The kiss?'

'No.'

'If you do and you want to keep it platonic, just colleagues, then that's fine. I won't push it. I understand.'

'I… No.'

Tanya watched the well-built man in front of her as he scrabbled around for words, embarrassed like a little schoolboy who had to talk about a kiss with the Prom Queen. She knew what she had to do.

Tanya stepped towards him and took one of his hands in hers. She could see the struggle playing in his mind and written on his face.

'Harrison,' she said. 'Harrison, look at me.'

He did as he was told and was instantly caught by the intensity of her blue eyes.

'Harrison, it's OK. I'm not going to take you away from who you are and what you need to do. I love everything about you. Your passion and your drive. And I think recent events would have shown you that I'm quite capable of taking care of myself. I'm not your mother, nothing's going to happen to me.'

Tanya stood on her tiptoes and kissed his lips. At first, they were unsure, but it didn't take her long before she found the passion she knew was there.

35

Harrison was late up the next morning. He'd slept so deeply that he'd turned off his alarm and consequently didn't get to New Scotland Yard until almost 10 a.m. All he could think about was Tanya and the evening they'd spent together, talking into the early hours, and the taste of her kisses.

As Harrison approached his office door, the sound of voices and laughter met him. At first he thought about going to get a drink, he wasn't in the mood for visitors, until he realised who it was behind the door, and a wave of relief spread through him. Today had just got a lot better.

Harrison pushed the door open to see the tall, broad bulk of Professor Andrew McKendrick filling the space between his desk and Ryan's. The latter was belly laughing at something the professor had just said. The pair turned to see Harrison like two naughty schoolboys caught up after lights out.

'Here he is.' The professor beamed a huge smile and opened his arms. Harrison didn't hesitate. He accepted the embrace with gratitude and warmth.

'Andrew, what a pleasure. It's been a while.'

'Yes, what's been keeping you away from my door? Not a certain young forensics officer, by any chance?'

Harrison sent a dagger'd look across to Ryan, who pretended to be studying something on his watch.

'No, work's been busy.'

'Good. They've realised your value, my boy. I told you they would.'

Harrison smiled at his old professor and mentor. 'You did indeed.' He remembered the night he'd gone round to his home, bemoaning the fact that they were calling him the Witch Hunter and the police detectives weren't taking him seriously. Andrew had told him then that all it would take was a handful of successes and word would spread. He'd been right.

'How have you been?' he asked. The professor looked a little weary, dare he say older than when he'd last seen him three months before. There were flashes of grey in his hair which he hadn't noticed before, and his usual rich black skin colour was looking lacklustre, as though it had lost its energy.

'I was attending a briefing on a case I consulted on years ago, before your time here. He's up for parole and apparently a reformed and cured man, but I'm not convinced. His doctors are adamant, but thankfully the officer who dealt with the case is of the same mind as me. We were coming up with a plan.'

'Do you want to grab something in the canteen?' Harrison asked.

'I would, but I have to be back for a lecture. Can we set a date for dinner?'

Both men consulted their phone diaries.

'How about next Thursday?' Andrew asked.

'Perfect.' Harrison added it to his calendar.

'And will I meet your new young lady?'

'She's not my young lady, it's early days,' Harrison replied, not sure what their relationship status was.

The professor changed the subject.

'I see you're still on the trail.' He nodded at

the photograph of Harrison's mother standing with Desmond and Freda Manning on his pin board. His face had grown serious, and he looked at Harrison as though trying to see beyond what was on his face.

'Yes. In fact, a detective has been helping me and we're making some headway. They are both alive. I saw them.'

'You saw them? When? Where?'

'They lured me to Nunhead Cemetery and then tricked me so they got away, but now I know they're still alive, I won't let that happen again.'

The professor had gone quiet and seemed to momentarily be lost for words.

'Are you feeling all right?' Harrison asked.

He studied his friend. It was always a pleasure seeing Andrew. He'd been like a father figure to him throughout university and afterwards. They'd found a kindred in the fact both of them had nearly gone off the rails in adolescence before finding their groove in life. Andrew had been abandoned as a child and in those days, it had been harder to find a suitable childless couple for a black child. In the end, a white couple fell in love with him and adopted him. They'd been wonderful parents, but it had been hard growing up as a black child with white parents. The bullying at school was bad enough because of his skin colour, but his family situation had made it relentless. He'd had to learn to be tough to survive. Luckily, he'd been tall and well built, so as he'd progressed through the years, fewer of the bullies were brave enough to challenge him. It left its scars, though. For a few years after school, he'd lost his way. He'd never told Harrison what had happened in those years, but when he'd first arrived in his tutor group like a fish out of water, the professor had recognised his struggle and given him wise counsel. They'd been best friends ever since.

Harrison hadn't seen him this quiet before. He wondered if there was something he needed to talk about, something that was troubling him.

'I'm fine. Just a bit tired after the early morning start. I don't want you getting hurt. People like the Mannings find a way to get to everyone, eventually. This reckoning has been a long time coming so you be careful.'

'I will.' Harrison smiled back at him, but he saw the change in Andrew's eyes.

'I'd better be off, or I'll have sixty students throwing things at each other in my lecture hall when they should be listening to me. I'll see you next week.'

Harrison watched his friend's back recede

down the corridor and wondered what the topic of their dinner conversation would be. In the meantime, he needed to get back to work. There were ritualistic crimes being committed, police detectives who needed his expertise, and victims who needed his help.

AFTERWORD

Firstly, a huge thank you for choosing to read The Horsemen. I hope you've enjoyed it. This series has been several years in the making and it's been an exciting experience to bring Harrison to the world. I would really appreciate it if you could leave a review on the Amazon book page. Reviews mean a lot to me as they do to all authors. They not only tell us that people are reading and appreciating our work, but it helps to guide other readers.

If you'd like to read a FREE short story about Harrison and DCI Barker's first case together, you can sign up for my Readers Club for free. I'll not bombard you with emails, but I'll keep you updated with release news, competitions, offers and more. Visit: GwynGB.com

Plus if you'd like to read more about Harrison and co, **Dark Order** is the third in the series.

As with all fiction, this book isn't based on any real people or practices in horseracing, although it was inspired by some actual events. However, The Horsemen societies, Toad men, Witch's bottles and objects placed inside the walls of houses for protection, were all once a part of British society folklore. Here are just two of the books that I used for research. If you'd like to do some further reading, I recommend them:

Witchcraft and Secret Societies of Rural England: The Magic of Toadmen, Plough Witches, Mummers, and Bonesmen by Nigel Pennick; and *Magical House Protection, The Archaelogy of Counter-Witchcraft* by Brian Hoggard.

Thank you again, I really do appreciate your support.

Best wishes

Gwyn

THANK YOU'S

Every book relies on a team of people and so I'd also like to say a few thank you's to those who have helped bring Book 2 in the Harrison Lane series to you. For the cover work, thank you to Adrijus from Rocking Book Covers. For her proof reading skills, thank you to my editor, Emma Mitchell at Creating Perfection who spots the inconsistencies and errors that inevitably creep into a book.

As always, my writing friends, The Blonde Plotters, Deborah and Kelly, who have provided so much moral support to me in writing this series. The life of a writer is a roller-coaster of emotion and it is wonderful to have great friends there to encourage you on. Thank you.

Finally, as always thanks to my husband and boys who have to put up with me having my head constantly stuck in my laptop; and of course Miss Molly, whose constant companionship keeps me going, and manages to drag me away long enough to get some exercise on our daily walks.

DARK ORDER

3RD IN THE HARRISON LANE MYSTERY SERIES

A UNIVERSITY SOCIETY TURNED DARK AND MURDEROUS

A PHANTOM MONK HAUNTING THE STREETS

CAN DR HARRISON LANE UNCOVER THE TRUTH BEFORE ANOTHER STUDENT DIES?

It all started off as a bit of fun, but somehow it ended with one of them dead. When the student friends attempt to hide the truth, it unleashes a sinister succession of events. The ghost of their dead friend starts to walk the streets of Durham city, risking the exposure of their secret, and bringing fear and ultimately murder.

Will Dr Harrison Lane, Head of the Ritualistic Behavioural Crime unit, be able to uncover the truth as he also battles to find out what happened in his own past?

Dark Order is the third in the Dr Harrison Lane mysteries, fast-paced crime suspense novels full of murder and intrigue, with a little romance and humour included. Harrison travels all over the British Isles as he solves the crimes hiding behind folklore, superstition, religion, and ritual.

ALSO BY GWYN

DI CLAIRE FALLE SERIES

LONELY HEARTS

Someone's watching. Someone's Lonely. Someone's going to Die. Could it be You?

Meet Rachel, she loves animals and works at a dating agency bringing lonely people together – only somebody is watching her every move and she's scared…

Neil didn't see who killed him – but his murder brings DI Claire Falle on the case. What she uncovers leads her to discover a serial-killer is preying on the clients of the dating agency where Rachel works.

Can Claire work out the connection between all the deaths before Rachel becomes the next victim?

What is it in Rachel's past that haunts her?

As DI Claire Falle investigates the lives of the dating agency staff and clients, she is pulled into a tangled web of loneliness and deceit which will have devastating consequences for someone...

What readers are saying about Lonely Hearts

"WOW - what a twist! It absolutely had me on the edge of my seat."

"Brilliant. If you want to get completely lost in a page-turner with an amazing twist, then Lonely Hearts is the book for you."

ABOUT GWYN GB

Gwyn GB is a writer living in Jersey, Channel Islands. Born in the UK, she moved there with her Jersey-born husband and their children. Gwyn has spent most of her career as a journalist, but has always written fiction in her spare time.

You can connect with Gwyn online:

Website: GwynGB.com

Printed in Great Britain
by Amazon

69775500R00196